The Inn

of

Beautiful Remains

RIAN ADARA

Book Cover by Drew Huff

Developmental Editing and Copyediting by Nico Bell and Tiffany Putenis

Formatting and Interior Design by Rian Adara

First Edition February, 2026.

ISBN: 978-0-9978743-8-9

For anyone who likes to push their own boundaries.

AUTHOR'S NOTE

Guys, this one's fucking weird. IDK. It's even more of an experiment than A Thing Divine was. The Inn of Beautiful Remains goes deeper into my dark psyche, and honestly, I'm not sure what I pulled out. But I guess we're on this ride together!

Something to keep in mind as you read, as Lucy's mind starts to unravel, the events of the book will grow more suspect, Lucy's perspective will become more unreliable, and the ending will leave you hanging. That's purposeful. And no, there is no second book. I dabbled with fragile sanity in A Thing Divine, but the outcome was clear-cut. That will not be the case here. If you do not like ambiguity, I recommend bowing out here.

Please keep in mind that this is an erotic horror novella. Emphasis on *horror*. Where A Thing Divine was able to exist on the fringes of dark romance, that is not the case with The Inn of Beautiful Remains. There is nothing romantic about this story. Not even a little bit. So please, read with caution.

This book contains swearing, heavy gore, gore play, blood play, graphic sex, consumption of menstrual blood, gaslighting, cannibalism, dubious consent (dubcon), nonconsensual sexual interactions (noncon), choking, night terrors, and captivity.

Little Sister's Inn is the perfect getaway for anyone who feels lost to find themselves in peace and serenity in the seaside town of Shadow Cove. Nestled on a wooded bluff overlooking the ocean, Little Sister's ~~bloody~~ bountiful history will surely ~~destroy~~ ease your mind just as her wonderful proprietor will ~~eat~~ capture your heart. With all the amenities you could possibly desire, Little Sister's is *the* destination to plumb the depths of your ~~corpse~~ soul to discover the true creature within. Once you check in, you may never want to leave.

Re: FWD: Thank You for Your Reservation at Little Sister's Inn!

To: QuinnMorrisEsq@helsinglaw.com
From: LucyWest87@nightshademail.com

Hey Luce,

I think the link you sent me broke, because I'm just getting a Page 404 when I click on it. I'm sure it's amazing, and you're finally going to get some time to chill out after everything you've been through.

I know, I know, I *know* you've turned me down a thousand times already, but I really wish you'd take up my offer to come with you. You really shouldn't be alone right now. And don't even. I can actually hear you roll your eyes. I said I *know*. I just want to support you as much as I can. I can work remotely, you know. 😏

Shadow Cove sounds creepy, but the tourism website I guess looks fine. The town looks quaint and cute, and it even has a fun little boardwalk where you can eat cotton candy until you puke! Most importantly, it looks chill. And I hope you chill while you're there.

Your parents might as well have been my parents growing up. That makes us sisters in all but blood. Which means I know you're putting on a grave face. The estate is settled, they're laid to rest, and now you need some time to decompress. I hope you get that at this doll house of an inn.

Send me updates. I require them. The more pictures of the ocean, the better as I'm stuck in my concrete cubicle hell.

Love you, doll,

Quinn 🩶

Thank You for Your Reservation at Little Sister's Inn!

I'M GOING TO DIE AT THIS AIRPORT.

It's not like San Jose is small, but I've been waiting forty-five minutes for someone to pick up my ride request. So far, no bites. I click my tongue as I move the map around in the CRGApp, looking at all the nearby drivers who keep ignoring my call. I have a forty percent tip average. What the hell is going on? Maybe I should have downloaded a different ride-share app before getting here.

This trip to a little out-of-the-way inn, in even more out-of-the-way Shadow Cove, California, was supposed to be some desperately needed downtime after . . . everything. Except now it's starting out with my impatience redlining after a long travel day. The fluorescent lights illuminating the pick-up area make the night sky beyond look even darker, and weariness settles heavier onto my shoulders. I just want to go to sleep.

At least check-in is late at Little Sister's Inn. Not sure I've ever seen a nine PM check-in before, but these small towns can be weird. It's already eight forty-five, and it's going to take forty-five minutes to get there. I hope that's not an issue. It's not like I can call them and confirm it'll be okay. They didn't provide a phone number.

I pull up the welcome email yet again. Maybe I missed it. Sure enough, as I scroll through all the lodging information, there's not a number to be found. I navigate to the website. Same thing. All their correspondence is through email or their contact form. At thirty, I know I'm not *that* old, but not even a phone number? I really hope I don't regret this trip, but I'd be lying to myself if I thought it was starting off good.

As I navigate back to the CRGApp, someone has *finally* accepted my ride request.

Five minutes out.

Thank fucking god.

A little bubble pops up with a tiny picture of the driver's face, and I tap on it. It takes me to the driver's screen, and I gasp when I get a look at the photo. Tanned skin and jet-black hair frame a sculpted face and piercing brown eyes that stare at me from within my phone. Right behind the shock of the good-looking man is a crawling sense of dread creeping up my spine. The more I look at the photo, the more unsettled I get. It's a feeling rearing up from the depths of me. Primal and instinctual. My skin prickles and I wiggle my shoulders as if to brush off the feeling. I take a deep breath, press my thumb between my eyebrows, and close my eyes, trying to shove the thoughts away. I don't use ride-share often. It goes against the whole notion of "don't get in a stranger's car" that was drilled into me growing up, and I can't seem to shake it.

Another breath shudders out, I open my eyes, and glance back at the screen. The four-point-seven out of five star rating sits underneath his photo, given to him from dozens of riders. The dread slowly oozes away and my breathing starts to steady.

The car he's driving is an old muscle car, a black, two-door something or other. Not the best choice for a ride-share car. I can only imagine what I'll look like trying to stuff myself in and out of the backseat. The thought cracks a smile across my tense face, and the dread evaporates.

I sigh heavily and drop my arm to my side. People come and go from the ride share loading area, and I breathe through my impatience. At least a ride is finally coming.

When the crowd lulls, headlights pierce through my vision, and the crack of thunder makes me jump. An engine roars, swallowing the boom that just rattled the cement corridor of the pick-up area. My heart is a jackhammer in my chest as I frown and quickly flip to my weather app. It was supposed to be clear the entire time I was here, but now a little cloud with a lighting bolt hovers over my evening forecast. A storm is coming.

The black vehicle rolls to a stop feet from me. I flip back to the CRGApp one more time to find that five minutes have, indeed, disappeared. I must be falling asleep on my feet.

I clear my throat, exhale the remnants of my anxiety and impatience, and plaster on some semblance of a smile. It's not this guy's fault. I don't want to be a bitch to him for being in the wrong place at the wrong time. This does appear to be my only chance at getting to Little Sister's tonight, after all. I don't want to screw it up by being a rider from hell.

The car door creaks as he unfolds himself from the car's interior and walks around the back of it. Ripped jeans and motorcycle boots paired with a fitted white T-shirt and an open button-down shirt more than compliment the gorgeous face from the app. Despite his spectacular appearance, dread seems to linger at the edges of my mind.

His gaze is piercing as it lands on me. It seeps through my skin and burrows into me, like he's studying a specimen. Part of me wants to grab my bags and recoil back into the terminal.

I'll get a different ride to a nearby hotel and figure everything out in the morning when the sun is bright and the shadows behind this man aren't so dark. The rest of me chastises me for being so stupid. My tired mind is making things up. Besides, I would feel horrible running off now.

"Easy enough to spot," he says with a nod in my direction.

I run my fingers through my hair out of habit. Naturally red hair this blazing, it's often easy enough to see me in a crowd. I'm about to say something about that until I glance to my left, then my right, and find nothing but empty sidewalk and closed terminal doors. I'm alone. Of course I'm easy to spot. Heat pulses in my cheeks and I swallow the embarrassment.

He reaches for my lone suitcase with little more than a blink, not acknowledging that I haven't responded. "Name's Aiden. Take the front seat."

As he passes the passenger side of the car he opens the door for me, revealing a black leather interior that blends seamlessly into the night. Dark bleeds into dark, creating a void within the car. Something that may absorb me entirely. The gear shift is indiscernible from the console which is indiscernible from the steering wheel. It is all one black mass. The darkness within is intimidating and total.

"You have to get in the car if you want me to take you to Shadow Cove," Aiden says, his voice flat.

I blink and find him looking at me over the roof of the car, his hand on the metal, finger tapping. My suitcase is gone, presumably in the trunk. Somewhere in the fog of my memory I hear the trunk thud closed, but the time between him reaching for my luggage and standing on the other side of the car is blank. Like the minute it took him to store my things didn't exist. Kind of like how waiting for him to arrive once he accepted my request felt like seconds, not minutes.

Jet lag and stress are really taking their toll. I press a knuckle into my temple and watch Aiden fold himself back into his car. When I peek inside again, the interior is just that. The interior of a car. Dirt and sand litter the mat in the wheel well. Dust coats the dash. The digital interface of a brand-new stereo system lights up the vintage surroundings. It's just a car.

Dread tickles the base of my spine once again, reminding me it's still lingering. I need this vacation too bad to let it drive off into the night now. I've come so far. The thought of asking Aiden to unload my bag and cancelling the ride swirls my stomach with shame. I'm too tired to deal with a stranger's disappointment. I came here to escape the disappointment of others, not run headlong into it.

"You've been waiting a while, right?" he asks, his voice flat. Leather creaks as he leans across the center console to peer at me. "And you're going to Little Sister's?"

I nod as I glance around the pick-up area. No cars drive through the lanes. No one stumbles out of the sliding glass doors with a bevy of suitcases in tow. Even the roar of planes is absent, leaving space for my heart to thunder in my ears. The world has stopped, waiting for me to finally make up my mind.

Not Aiden nor the CRG ride or the seemingly abandoned airport bode well for the start of my trip, and I seriously consider whether I should actually heed the warnings the universe is trying to give me. Back away, abandon my original plans, and find something safer in the more populated city.

"You're not going to get another ride. Not many people are willing to go all the way out there from here. Too far. And—"

His mouth moves, but the words stop. His lips close, and he tilts his head to the side as if waiting for me to respond.

"And . . .?" I ask, encouraging him to finish his thought.

He shakes his head and lifts a single shoulder. "Too far. Roads aren't great. It's me or nothing."

"Why you?" I ask him, as I place my hand on the door. "Of all people, you?"

The intimacy of the question pulls me up short. I can't believe that just came out of my mouth. As if the words skipped my brain and found my tongue all on their own. Heat blares on my cheeks, but I keep myself as steady as possible despite the sweat beading on the back of my neck.

He lifts his shoulder again, his dark brown eyes drilling holes into me. "I live in Shadow Cove. You got lucky. I was running errands. You getting in or what? I don't got all night."

A little voice, hardly louder than the squeak of a mouse, tells me to go back into the terminal. My legs twitch, ready to carry me away from Aiden, his car, and even my suitcase currently residing in his trunk. I can replace everything in there, anyway. My purse is strapped across my body. That's all I need.

No.

What I *need* is this trip. I've been desperate for it. To leave everything behind. Every obligation, every expectation left back home for someone else, or no one else, to deal with. Ever since I graduated college, I've been living for other people. Reaching for *their* dreams, aspiring to hit *their* goals. I've been successful, sure. But I've also been . . . empty. My parents' deaths broke me out of the fugue state I've been living in. It woke me up, and now I need some time away from the expectations of me to figure out who I even am.

Still, the desire — the *need* — to not make waves, to just acquiesce despite what my gut says, is at a peak. Asking Aiden to take my luggage back out and to leave me here means inconveniencing him. Despite this trip being for me, I just can't shake the habit of swallowing my own discomfort for the sake of others, and I hate myself for it.

Something plays on the radio, but the music is turned down so far I can't make out what it is. With a hard swallow, I place one foot in the wheel well and lower myself inside. Just as I dip below the roof of the car, I catch a smirk tilt up the corner of Aiden's mouth. A chill wraps around my throat as I lose my control and plop into the seat, shaking the car in the process. By the time I close the door, Aiden's smirk is gone, and his hands wrap around the steering wheel. His stoic face is back on as if it never left.

We pull away from the curb, and dread fills my stomach. My phone screen lights up the interior with the map from the CRGApp displaying our moving little red dot, my sole comfort that something is keeping an eye on me, even if that something is nothing but code. Aiden says nothing to me about it, or anything else. So, I watch our route track on the app, moving toward Little Sister's Inn.

As we move through the city, the world is bright, a hazy orange dotted with headlights. The freeway is wide and well lit. But sooner rather than later we move off the main thoroughfare and onto a windy mountain road that twists and turns through trees so dense it's nothing but black around us. Until a bolt of lightning streaks across the sky, lighting up the leaves just before a crack of thunder rumbles over the sound of the revving engine. I flinch despite myself, the bolt leaving flickering afterimages in my vision. Yet another reminder that my previously weather-free, calm trip is being upended by nature not caring about my plans.

"Sounds like a storm is moving in." Aiden's voice is a rumble of a different tenor, vibrating through the seats and shaking the marrow in my bones.

I glance at him from the corner of my eye, but he stares

straight ahead. He slouches with one hand on the steering wheel, his fingers barely touching it. As if the car drives itself.

Other cars taper off until we're the only one on the narrow, winding road, zipping around turns and streaming down hills like we're on a racetrack. We drive through darkness with nothing but our headlights cutting through the night. I don't know how much time passes before I realize it must have been miles since I've seen another car. It's just me and a stranger rushing through a void.

When the silence grows unbearable, punctuated only by the muted tones wafting out of the speakers, and the air feels like a leaded weight on my shoulders, I let the words hovering at the back of my throat tumble out. "I don't think I realized the hotel was so rural."

Aiden huffs, and the corner of his mouth curls. If it weren't for his brusque tone and sharp stare, I'd find him attractive. More than attractive.

"It's dark. Everything is worse in the dark."

The hairs on the back of my neck stand on end.

I turn to him and ask, "Worse? What do you mean, worse?" I try to keep my voice as even as I can, but my hand grips my phone so hard my knuckles ache.

"Rural," he says, as he looks at me with one raised eyebrow. Then he motions out the pitch-black window with his chin. "This ain't rural. Just looks it in the dark. People say they're afraid of the dark, but it ain't the dark they're afraid of. It's what's in it that terrifies them."

Normal drivers ask where I'm from, what my plans are, what movies I've seen recently. Instead, my CRG driver's small talk includes things in the dark I should be afraid of. No, that doesn't bode well at all.

I glance at my app again and see we still have another fifteen minutes before we get there. Yet again I find myself questioning my decisions. The app says we're fine. We're exactly where we should be. But my nagging doubt tells me I shouldn't have ignored my growing misgivings that just seem to keep growing no matter how much sense I try throwing at them. A flash of heat rushes down my back, and sweat clings under my arms, yet I have to bite my tongue to keep my teeth from chattering. Perhaps if I keep him talking it'll distract him —and me—from the emptiness we seem to be hurtling through.

"Are people afraid of these woods?" I ask him, swallowing the shudder in my voice.

"Petrified," he says with another smirk that chills the blood in my veins.

I swallow hard and ask, "Why's that?" I move my finger to the volume button on my phone, ready to rapid press it to trigger an emergency call, only to notice my service hovers around a single bar. Fuck.

He looks at me again, taking his eyes off the road as we round a sharp turn without a single tap on the brakes. As if he knows this road and can drive it in his sleep. "You didn't look into this place at all, did you?"

My heart races as nearby leaves slap along the side of the car, the vehicle coming perilously close to the edge of the road. Fear clenches my throat as my thoughts muddle. His dark gaze drills into me for what feels like an age.

"Of course I did," I whisper, shame heating my cheeks as I feel the need to defend myself and my decisions despite my own feelings about them. "Was I supposed to find something beyond reviews and tourism articles about Shadow Cove?"

There's a bite to my response, edged with annoyance. I didn't come here to do research or look into local lore or whatever Aiden is getting at. I came to Shadow Cove to chill the fuck out, and right now I'm feeling the exact opposite.

Aiden shrugs. "I guess not."

"No," I tell him, as I shake my head. "You don't get to be smug and bait me about Shadow Cove. Is there something I should know about it or not?"

"No. There isn't," he says before he turns his eyes back to the road. "Just bad dreams people can't get over. You'll do just fine."

Something deep and primal tells me not to bite back at a man who effectively holds me hostage in his car in the middle of nowhere with no cell phone service. It's a recipe for a horror movie. But I can't help it. Whatever reservations I had about ruffling feathers fritters away. I'm annoyed. I looked into Shadow Cove and Little Sister's. I found nothing beyond what a quaint little beach town it is and the four and a half stars the inn has. Forty-five minutes from San Jose, maybe an hour south of San Francisco, it's hardly in the middle of nowhere. Yet this man—Aiden—insinuates there's something I should know. Or he's fucking with me for the hell of it. I'm not about to tolerate that either.

He huffs and licks his lips, the movement drawing my eyes to his mouth. I get a peek of gleaming white teeth as his lips close again. A moment passes before he glances at me, a quick look and back to the road. Yet I've never felt more exposed by a look. His eyes remain glued to the road, but a gaze like fire travels down my body all the same. It feels like a finger running down my chest, my navel, to the crook between my legs, and back up. I glance out my window, but only my own reflection looks back. Nothing else looks at me. Nothing I can see, anyway.

This man is terrifying. He exudes something predatory. Deadly. I should be clawing my way out of his car. Still, I remain, nothing but the pounding of my heart giving me some semblance of solace. It tells me at least I'm still alive.

My jaw aches from clenching it. A stylized *Welcome to Shadow Cove* sign grows in the distance, emerging from the shadows as if pushing through a curtain. My muscles relax, if only a fraction. I didn't realize we'd moved out of the mountain roads during our less-than-appealing conversation and are now making our descent into the beach town.

Despite how fast we drive, the sign appears to lumber past. There are supposed to be two spotlights lighting up the sign, but only one works. The other flickers at erratic intervals, slashing black gouges across the smiling faces of the people in the mural. Tags and designs speckle the frame. Lots of skulls and RIPs. It's a stark contrast to the bright, sunny beach day the image depicts.

It isn't until the welcome sign is disappearing behind us that I fully realize what Aiden said. *I'll do just fine.* Just fine at what? I want to ask him about it, demand he clarify, but streetlights and a seemingly quiet little town blanketed in an oppression of fog demand my attention. Finally, civilization. I glance at my phone, but my service still hovers at a single bar that flashes in and out.

We drive through what could pass for a vintage picture, dull yellows from the streetlights painting an aesthetic wash over everything, aided by store signs that look like they're out of the seventies, hand-painted designs punctuated with swirls of neon lights. The clock on the dash tells me it's close to ten and it shows. Clothing shops, an ice cream parlor, restaurants, and an old-fashioned diner line the road. All dark, locked up and silent for the night. The smell of brine and sun-cooked sand filter through the vents the closer we get to the water. If I didn't know any better, I could convince myself it smells like rot, not the beach. Like something left out too long. Something forgotten.

Low-lying clouds hover over the town, peeking around

building corners, swirling through alleys. The town could either be asleep or abandoned for how quiet it is.

"Is it always this . . . dead?" I whisper but don't mean for it to come out that low. My fear of Aiden and how unnerving that welcome sign was dissolve in the face of Shadow Cove. They are nothing compared to the ghost town we drive through. A dead town that was supposed to be very much alive. "Where is everyone?"

We take a turn, and the radio's music wafts over to me in a dissonant wail before it goes quiet again, fading into the background. My doubts about my choices that got me here—in this car with Aiden, driving through an empty Shadow Cove— come roaring back. Where I wanted to get out of the car before, now I want to cower from the doors. Lean into Aiden for protection from the graveyard of a world outside.

"Shadow Cove is a small town, and tourist season is over. Things close up early. That's all," Aiden says, his voice low and guttural.

We turn again, this time down an overlook road. The guardrail and the edge of the cliff are visible, but nothing beyond that. What I assume is the ocean has been smudged out of existence.

The road narrows the further we drive. Still two lanes, but barely. This beast of a car must surely be riding the center line, but Aiden navigates the lane as if he has it memorized. Which he should, since he lives here. Or so he says.

"And the fog?" I ask, as headlights slice through the murk. "Is this normal? I don't think I've ever seen fog like this."

"You seem too concerned about normal. Why?" he returns instead of answering my question.

It causes me to sit up straight and frown as I mull the question over. I haven't forgotten about the fog, but this feels personal. Intrusive. Yet I feel compelled to answer.

"I just . . ."

My life has always been so rigid and organized. Dictated for me, from my choice of college, to my career path, to where I went to work. There have been expectations of me, and because I was born to please, taught that there were no other options but to do as I was told, it's what I did. My parents' deaths, as tragic as they were, and as upsetting, has been a relief. But I'm also a little bit . . . lost. With the strings cut and me alone making my own decisions for once, I feel pulled in a million different directions. Settling into an old routine is where I find comfort. Only now it's time to find new comforts. Not that I'll tell Aiden any of that.

"I want this to be a good trip. I've been through a lot lately, and I just want to relax."

Aiden waits a beat, perhaps giving me the chance to elaborate, but I won't. That's as personal as he's going to get out of me. When he must realize that, he nods and shifts in his seat.

"Mina will give you exactly what you need." Aiden looks at me from the corner of his eye.

I want to think he means it as uplifting, but I can't help but hear the sinister thread embroidering his words. The hint of warning behind it. Maybe I'm just being paranoid. I am clearly on edge. My hands fist in my lap and I release them, the sweet sharpness of pain flashing up my arms before it fizzles into nothing.

"You know the proprietor of Little Sister's?" I ask, my voice shaky. I try to swallow my weakness, but I find it a rock settled on the back of my tongue.

Aiden lifts his finger and circles it before looking back at the road. "Small town, remember? And it's normal."

"What is?" I ask, confused.

"The fog. Rolls in every night before it rolls right on out

again. You'll be hard up to catch a sunset here, especially this time of year," he adds.

"Oh." I don't know what else to say.

Instead, I stare out the window, watching the town roll by in closed-up clumps of stores and restaurants. Lights behind glass give the illusion of something being open, but that's all it is. Illusion.

We take another turn, and the ocean opens up in front of us, the white caps visible among the black waters smothered by a thinner layer of fog. To our left a small amusement park lights up the night, a beacon in an otherwise dead town. Flickering lights race along the track of an old wooden rollercoaster, and circus-tent-like roofs dot along a small boardwalk. Contraptions spin, and in the lull of the music I hear the rolling screams of riders.

"Not everything is closed up for the night," I say. I sit up as he rolls along the cliff's edge, houses lining the other side of the road.

"No," Aiden says and leaves it at that.

The structures on the road become more residential, old homes leaning against the ocean wind. In the middle of it all sits a squat building with a neon 'open' sign stuck in its window. What looks like its only window. The door opens and the ancient whines of a jukebox tune waft out behind a startlingly attractive man.

Black boots with lean black jeans, a gray shirt, and red field jacket complete his look. Simple. Like Aiden. But where Aiden's complexion is dark, this man is light, yet far from angelic. A hard-lined jaw carries days-old scruff as piercing eyes find mine in the dark. I stifle a gasp and push myself deeper into the seat.

The man places a cigarette between his lips. The flame from the lighter flares against his face, lighting his features like a haunt in the shadows before there's nothing left except the smolder of burning paper and tobacco. Cigarettes are deeply unpleasant. Their smell putrid. In any other situation I wouldn't give the man a second thought, but right now, I find I can't look away. It isn't until the little dive bar sits too far behind us that I look back out the windshield and give the drive the rest of my attention.

The road snakes along the ocean front, battered by waves below us, until the headlights reveal the edge of the paved road and the beginning of a trail of dirt. Whatever houses were around were left behind. Nothing but trees and ocean surround us now. He rolls to a stop at the end of the paved road and puts the car in park.

"This is it." He opens his door, the pop of the trunk a thunk inside the car.

"Excuse me?" I look at my phone. Sure enough the destination should be right around here, but it's nothing but blackness on the other side the windshield. This has to be a joke.

"Mina doesn't like folks on her property without an invitation. It's just up the hill there. You'll survive." His voice hitches as he lifts the suitcase and places it on the ground next to the tire.

"I thought you knew her? You can't just leave me here. What am I supposed to do? Drag my stuff through the dirt?" I try to keep the squeal out of my voice, but I'm afraid I'm failing.

Sweat beads on my upper lip and under my arms as panic rises in my veins. This can't be happening.

"Stop making a big deal of it. Does that thing show you being here?" Aiden motions to the phone I hold in my hand.

I look at it as if ordered. Just like a moment ago, it shows we're practically standing on top of Little Sister's. It really must be at the end of this horrifying, pitch-black back road.

"Yes," I mutter, my voice quiet as I look back up at him. "Please, just take me to the door. I'll pay you extra."

"Told you," he says, as he slides back into the driver's seat and shuts his door. "Mina doesn't like people on her property who aren't invited. And I ain't invited. Go on. You'll thank me when you get there."

His headlights blind me as he pulls back and turns his car around. Tires press against the pavement in a susurration as the gears change, and he drives back the way we came. Taillights are two red eyes glaring at me from the growing darkness before they wink out completely.

2

THE ROAR OF THE OCEAN SOMEWHERE BEYOND THE cliffs is a flick at an exposed nerve. Despite the noise it makes, my boots shuffling along the dirt are a cacophony. I take deep, heaving breaths as I death-grip my phone in one hand and grab my suitcase with the other. The fog settles like a low ceiling over my head, wiping out the tops of the trees. There's no light haze to make the clouds glow. I turn my cell phone flashlight on, and I can barely see a matter of feet in front of me, the darkness and the fog are so thick.

An animal chitters, followed by the short barks of something canine. My heart rockets into my chest. My gaze dashes around the unpaved road, but there's nothing to see. A branch cracks somewhere in the smudge beyond. I jump, my heart racing. My sweaty fingers wrap around the handle of my suitcase. I take one purposeful step in front of the other and make my way down the lane.

My one saving grace is the single, flickering bar of service I still have, for whatever that's worth, and the map guiding my way. Another branch breaks, and a shrill cry pierces the night.

I whip my phone around and shine a light at the side of the road. Little more than fog reflects back at me, until I point the light back the way I came.

Two piercing red reflections catch the glare, there and gone in an instant. Just an animal, I remind myself. A stray cat, maybe. I move the beam back toward me and gasp as it catches another set of glowing red eyes. Closer than the ones before. I swallow hard and keep walking, the crunch of my boots in the gravel loud in the dead, dark quiet.

The beam moves ahead of me, bouncing with my steps. I shriek and stumble back, abandoning my luggage in my panic. Golden eyes with jet-black pupils and bloodshot whites stare into the beam of light. Into me. My phone slips from my hand and hits the dirt with a thud. I snatch it back up with shaking hands and point the light back at the beast only to find nothing there. Something howls, and the hairs on the back of my neck stand on end. I grab my luggage once again and tug it along, keeping closer to the ocean side of the road and away from where the eyes were. I pick up my pace, not wanting to push my luck with the local wildlife.

Normally a gentle lull, the roar of the ocean is now a reminder of demise. One wrong step and I could slip off the edge and tumble into its arms. But the other side of the road contains something living. Watching. Waiting. I would gladly welcome the water's cold embrace over that.

Before long, the road turns away from the unseen cliff's edge. Wrought iron lampposts emerge from the soupy air, their muted haze a welcome sight in the smothering night. The small cones of light don't travel far, but it's enough to hold the fog at bay, and I thank the inclement Shadow Cove weather for the reprieve.

The app says I'm nearly there. When I look up from my phone I gasp and lurch back. A giant, black, wrought iron gate looms over me only a couple feet away. Another step and a half and I would have gone face first into the ornate M swirled into the center. My cheeks flame at the embarrassment I just avoided.

A piercing red light catches my eye. I turn my head and brace myself for another prying animal, only to find an intercom system. A stylized note is taped to the box telling guests to ring for entry.

Calm yourself, Luce.

Shame floods through me at my fear and my reactions to everything since arriving. At my anxiety. I just want to crawl into bed and forget this day even happened.

I stab the button, and a subtle buzz sounds in the speaker. I look around, trying to spot cameras but see nothing. The gate clicks and the arms swing wide, breaking the M in half and allowing me entrance. No voice comes over the intercom. No instructions. I assume that means I enter. I'm not sure who else this woman, Mina, could be expecting, but I know for a fact she's expecting me. I have the email confirmation to prove it.

As if the gates push back the fog, another bolt of lightning slices across the sky, casting a spotlight on the Victorian inn, and thunder rumbles in the distance. For a moment, Little Sister's looms in front of me, dilapidated and weather worn. Shingles are missing from the roof. Windows are broken. No lights beam from the interior. As soon as the lightning finishes its arc, the inn settles back into shadows, the stubborn fog still lingering. My tired, jet-lagged mind wrestles with what I think I just saw and immediately files it away as tricks of the light and exhaustion.

As I enter the property, the driveway opens up and the fog fades, revealing more of the same wrought iron streetlights. The well-lit path gives me permission to leave my unsettling

CRG ride and the haunting night behind me. With each step I take, the fog clears more, revealing not a stormy night sky but a clear night speckled in stars. As if the heavens only shine for Little Sister's. Dark shrubs that line the walkway are crisp and clear. Nothing like the ominous overgrown vegetation on the side of the unpaved road. Trees hang over me as their leaves rustle in the light breeze, and the shush of the ocean in the distance gently strokes the fear and anxiety from my soul.

I shriek as the gate squeals closed behind me, but when I turn the fog is gone. As if it was never there at all. The lights dotting the driveway reach beyond the gate and curve with the unpaved road. Lights that were not there moments ago. I frown and take a step back to the gate, my mind yet again wrestling with what it's seeing. What I know, for a fact, was not there as I approached the property. I look at my phone and find the flashlight still lit, beaming onto my shoes. Proof that it was dark enough to be needed. As my thoughts try to form into something coherent, a voice jolts me into the present.

"You must be Lucy!"

I spin around, my hair swirling with the movement. The thump of feet on wooden stairs draws my eyes further up the driveway and to the monstrous Victorian settled atop a small hill at the back of the property. Artistically hidden lights shine on dollhouse siding and gables, making the house a beacon in the dark. One I should have seen even from the poorly lit lane I walked to get here. I press a finger into the corner of my eye and rub the exhaustion away as best I can. I honestly don't think I've ever been this tired.

A figure moves down the massive wrap-around porch and across the driveway to greet me.

"Welcome!" she says, as she draws closer.

At first I'm annoyed by just about everything. By the required late check-in. By waiting so long at the airport for a ride. By Aiden dumping me so far from the house. By the mindfuck of a walk I just took. But when I get a look at the woman coming to greet me, all my anger and irritation disappears like the fog.

"I'm Mina. I hope it wasn't too much trouble getting here," she says with warmth in her voice.

She reaches out a hand. Her warm fingers wrap around mine before I realize my hand is even out for hers to take. For a moment I'm simply lost in *her*. She's my height, but the messy mop of curly hair on top of her head adds a solid four inches. Her skin is dark against mine, a tawny brown to the sharp paleness of my own. Thick, well-crafted eyebrows sit above deep brown eyes, and her white smile beams out of full, luscious lips. Her grip is firm, her arms muscular, but a lot of her body is otherwise hidden under flowing palazzo pants with snake-like designs swirling up the legs and a haphazardly cropped shirt with jagged edges kissing the waistline. Bare feet poke out of the pant legs as she wraps her fingers around my arm and takes my suitcase from me.

I try to gather my thoughts, desperate to make sense of the whiplash the start to this trip has given me, but Mina's presence is a balm. I find I have a hard time focusing on anything but her.

"I know the check-in time can be a pain in the ass, but it's just me here, so it's a necessity. My days are tied up elsewhere, and I can't be in multiple places at once, you know?" She guides me along the path, among blooming flowers shedding their fragrance in the night air and something skittering among the shrubs.

Whatever fear I had, whatever concerns, Mina has just melted them away. If it's just her in this old house in the middle of nowhere in a small, nothing town, no wonder she doesn't want strangers coming onto her property. No wonder the gate is barred, and she has to unlock it from the house. She's just protecting herself. It makes perfect sense.

"It's fine," I tell her. She guides me through the pristine front garden and up the porch stairs lit from inside through the open front door. The house is a looming specter, but it radiates warmth with Mina on my arm. "It looks lovely."

She beams and adds a skip to her step as she tightens her grip on my arm. "I try. It's a lot of work. You can get a better look at it in the morning, but I'm proud of it."

We walk inside, and I have to dodge a nearby ladder with someone standing over my head. My gaze travels up the metal rungs to find a bronzed man in a cut-off shirt with lean, muscled arms reaching toward wiring sticking out of the wall. A curly mop of dirty blond hair sits thick on top of his head, long enough to curl around his ears.

"Sorry, Owen. I had to greet my guest," Mina says and motions to me.

I smile awkwardly.

When he turns to look over his shoulder I'm pinned to the floor under his piercing gaze. Deep blue eyes stare out of a young face that I know, deep in my gut, is far from young. His tool belt sits low on his hips. He absently lifts it as he drags his gaze to Mina.

"I get it," he says to her before turning that stare on me. "Enjoy your stay." There's no warmth in his tone and no smile on his face.

Not that I expected a welcome parade from an electrician, but Owen carries the same aura as Aiden. Dire, brooding, and aloof. It must be the town.

Mina looks at me and shrugs. "Another downside to not being available during the day, I have to have work done at night. Don't worry. There won't be any noise to keep you up."

"Am I the only guest?" I stare around an interior that leans into its Victorian roots.

Lots of wainscoting and crown molding, wood floors, and ornate accessories mingle with a flatscreen TV, a bookshelf of books and games, and a Kurig coffee maker. It's gorgeous, if not anachronistic. And a whole lot perfect. My anxiety lessens with each step, Mina's warm welcome and the cozy interior of Little Sister's exactly what I need after the long, taxing day I had getting here.

"You are," she says, as she leads me up the stairs. "It's the off season and business is slow. You'll have the whole place to yourself. I only have a few rules."

Framed pictures and newspaper articles slide past in a blur of yellowed paper and gilt frames as Mina guides me up the staircase. I catch a garish headline about a train crash and death and try to do a double take, but my feet carry me forward, my body eager to follow Mina even if my mind hasn't caught up yet.

We reach the landing, smaller than I was anticipating. A lit hallway to my right beckons me, while the dark hallway to my left grows darker by the second. No lights dot the walls on that side of the floor, and the ambient light from the landing and stairs hardly reaches the first couple of doors. I squint, trying to see through the haze of shadows, just as something flutters and disappears behind a cracked-open door. A piece of fabric, maybe. Or a white hand.

A clearing throat snaps me out of my trance. Mina stands next to me with waiting eyes and a comforting smile. We hover in front of a door I don't remember walking toward to what I assume will be my room. She looks at me with a quirked eyebrow.

I shake the shadowy images out my head and give Mina my

full attention while the pulsing darkness over her shoulder tries to draw my gaze like an eager child.

"Of course," I tell her, my nerves rattling under her stare.

She points behind her. "Stay out of the way of the workers. Their time is limited. It's best not to bother them at all."

I nod as I glance at the electrician, Owen, still visible from around the bend in the grand staircase. He catches my eye and heat flushes my body as he looks away. I quickly look back at Mina.

"Locked doors stay locked. You are the only guest, but it's a matter of my privacy and your safety. You understand, of course," she says, as she motions to me. I nod.

"Good," she says with a smile. "I'm having a lot of work done. Exposed wiring and such. You know how it is."

Intricate patterns on the damask wallpaper swirl and throb, the walls breathing in tune with my own breaths. Each inhale twists the designs and each exhale unknots them, returning them to their original pattern. In that moment, my exhaustion hits me. My weary bones feel the call of the bed just on the other side of the door, and I desperately want to answer it. My anxiety, my weariness, my fear all drains from me, leaving me spent.

"And lastly, respect the night."

The wallpaper has me hypnotized when Mina's words jolt me. They rattle around in my head for a moment before they settle into something understandable, yet I don't quite understand.

"I'm sorry?" I say.

Mina smiles and rests a hand on my bicep, her touch warm and comforting. "Shadow Cove is a beautiful place, but you must show it respect, especially once the sun goes down. You saw the fog, yes?"

I nod.

"Get lost in that and you'll walk right off the cliff's edge. Not to mention the predators that call these woods home." She brushes my hair over my shoulder and trails her fingers down my back. "They'll take one look at you and want to gobble you up."

For a moment I think I see Mina's eyes flash, only to have a flickering candle in my periphery draw my attention.

"Mountain lions, bobcats, wolves. It's dangerous out there. If you do venture out at night, be careful. Or I can escort you, if that's something you want." Mina's mouth softens as she stares at my face. I swallow hard under her look.

I've been dogpiled by people for the last handful of months as I managed my parents' funeral and estate. I haven't had a moment to myself. That was the whole point of this trip. Go somewhere out of the way and secluded to be alone. As I stand here in front of Mina, being alone becomes less desirable. Maybe a little time in her company could be what I really need.

"I might like that," I tell her with a small nod and a smile.

"Fantastic." She beams. "I'll leave you to it this evening, and the day will be yours tomorrow. I'll be away, of course. The kitchen is at the back of the house. Help yourself to anything you find there. Explore the grounds, explore the town. We'll reconvene tomorrow evening, and I'll answer any questions you have. Sound good?"

I nod, stunned at her hospitality. I've always been taken care of but never like this. Never with it being about *me*. A knot of tears grows thick in my throat, and I swallow it down, trying to keep my eyes from pooling. Quinn has been the only person who looked out for me for my sake in so long. Now with Mina, this stranger doing it as well, the relief of it all overwhelms me.

"There's water, a coffee brewer, and a water boiler in the

kitchen always stocked with coffee and tea should you want it. Is there anything else I can get you?"

I shake my head, my heart fluttering. It's so much and so nice I could collapse in her arms and weep with thanks. "No. This is wonderful, thank you."

"Have a good night, Lucy." Mina grazes her hand down my arm and carries herself back to the first floor.

The key sits heavy in my hand. An actual key. Metal tinkles against metal as I seat it in the lock, and the dark hallway draws my attention once again. With my fingers wrapped around the key, I stand still, waiting for any movement. Mina and Owen chatter downstairs as the shuffling of life carries on. There are no floorboard creaks or doors clicking shut. I can just make out a gilded frame at the far end of the dark hallway and the pale outlines of doorjambs. At the farthest door, something slides along the wood. Something long and finger-shaped before it disappears into a room. As if someone realized I could see their hand, and they drew it back.

Mina said I'm the only guest. She also said she's the only one who runs the inn, which would mean Owen is for hire.

I sigh and press a finger to the corner of my eye and rub the tension away. I'm tired. Exhausted. The weight of the world and my worries have been lifted from my shoulders. I should feel free, but right now I just want to sleep. My mind is playing tricks on me, and I'm not in the mood to abide it.

I turn the key and the door releases, opening to a grand room every bit as ornate as the house I just walked through. A cold fireplace sits on one side and a massive four-poster bed centers the wall opposite it. Between the two are floor-to-ceiling glass doors that overlook what I guess is the back of the inn. In the morning I'll see what my view truly is.

For now, my travel weighs heavy on me, and this giant bed looks too inviting to resist. I pull what I need to get ready for bed from my luggage, leaving the rest until morning. A quick shower to wash the day away makes me feel human again until I look in the mirror and find the wear these last months have caused. My stringy hair sits knotted on top of my head, dull and desperate for a trim and a deep conditioning. My eyes appear sunken with how dark my bags are, and the corners of my mouth turn down in a tired pout. The stark lighting isn't doing my skin any favors, making it look sallow, even sickly.

I flick the light off and walk back into the bedroom, trying not to let my exhausted self take up too much of my worries. The cool sheets of a tightly made bed are an embrace as I allow the four-poster to wrap its arms around me. It gives me permission to relax. For the first time since getting on the plane, something within me releases. Unclenches. It feels divine.

Faces swirl in my mind. Aiden and Owen and Mina flash through my thoughts, stuck there like flies on sticky paper. Sharp gazes and curt interactions soften against Mina's gentle touch and her welcoming demeanor. My skin burns where her fingers grazed, where her hand rested, and I pull the sheet tighter around my shoulders.

I close my eyes as my head settles into the lush pillow. Sleep pulls me down, but as I'm sinking the creak of a floorboard sends me shooting back to the surface. My eyes fly open, but I only have the strength to hold them open for a moment. Exhaustion is stronger as it drags me back down. I may hear another creak—the last thing I remember before sleep takes me—but I'm too tired to care.

Re: Re: FWD: Thank You for Your Reservation at Little Sister's Inn!

To: LucyWest87@nightshademail.com
From: QuinnMorrisEsq@helsinglaw.com

Q,

Finally here! What a mess to get here, but I'm here. I must have picked an off time to come because it took a thousand years to get a ride to town. When I did, I thought I was going to end up dead on the side of the road. My CRG driver would have been enjoyable to look at it if he wasn't so creepy. I'll tell you more about him the next time I see you. So far, this trip is doing a great job of taking my mind off of everything. If nothing else, it's a distraction.

Mina, the proprietor, is lovely and it turns out I'm the only one here. Hooray for having an entire Victorian mansion to myself for the week! I'm such a sucker for old houses. You know there's history here. There always is. I promised myself I'd do only mindless things, but the temptation to dig into this house might be too much. There were some old articles framed on the walls. I doubt I'll be able to stop at just reading those.

Apparently, the night will kill me, but what's a small beach town without some urban legends? Mina was saying the fog has gotten people turned around, and they've walked off of nearby cliffs. Or there are mountain lions or other gruesome predators that eat people. The welcome sign into town was tattooed with weird graffiti. But the boardwalk looks fun enough, and Mina offered to take me one night.

I know. I can hear you from here. I'm willing to spend time with Mina, a complete stranger, but I told you I wanted to be alone. She offered as she was walking me to my room. What was I supposed to do? Say no? Plus she's . . . alluring and hires equally alluring contractors. 😉 Who knows? Perhaps this is the kind of vacation I actually needed! I can hear your bark of laughter from here. I know I'm a wreck in that department, but maybe Mina and her hired hands will break me of that.

Don't worry. You'll be the first I tell should anything happen.

Talk soon.
🖤 Luce

3

I sleep like the dead and wake in the late morning. Sun pours through the sheer curtains on the balcony doors, and I wince against its brightness. A hard turn from the fog of the night before. I pull myself from the bed and stretch my back before I stand and make my way to the balcony. I didn't sleep with any windows open last night, but as I throw open the doors and feel the chill ocean breeze wash over me that may likely change tonight. The room was a little stuffy and stagnant. Now, I close my eyes as I revel in the breeze and the sun warming my skin.

From Little Sister's perch atop of the cliffs, the sleepy beachside community of Shadow Cove sprawls before me. A low haze hangs over the town like a gossamer blanket, smudging out homes while allowing the wooden spines of the rollercoaster to break through.

The air around the house is clear and crisp. Dew glitters on the grass in the yard as the climbing sun washes across it. Such a stark contrast to the Shadow Cove, and Little Sister's, of the night before. My tired, anxious mind was surely playing tricks on me.

The door stays open as I make quick work of getting dressed, eager to get out and explore. See what the town really has to offer other than deadly quiet nights. I know Mina said I'm alone in this house, but the shifting shadows of the night before are still fresh in my mind. I could have sworn I saw someone at the other end of the hall. But even as I stand at the top of the ornate staircase and look down the deserted corridor, there's nothing that would tell me anyone else is here. The doors are all closed. There are no lights to illuminate the hallway. Not even any muffled rustling from inside any of the rooms. I appear to be truly alone.

Little Sister's is bright during the day. Morning sun streams through the windows, washing everything in an uplifting glow that gives me new perspective on this trip. After last night, such a horrible start was bound to be a portent for what was to come. That feels less so now. Granted, everything seems brighter and more optimistic in the light of day.

As I make my way down the stairs, I take note of the frames on the wall, little more than blurs last night. Now they're fully formed, old pictures from a century ago or more. Sepia-colored photos holding dour-looking faces all stare back at me, watching me move down each step.

Just above the first floor landing is a framed newspaper article from the late 1800s detailing a train accident. This must have been the headline I caught last night. I move closer, trying to read the tiny font despite having no trouble with the garishly large headline:

SEASIDE TRAIN CRASH KILLS ALL ABOARD

A tragic day for Shadow Cove as residents mourn the loss of indi-

viduals they didn't know: travelers to their quaint seaside town, families, perhaps potential friends whose relationships will never bloom. The Trans-Pacific Rail, the line newly built just a year prior, flew from its tracks. Investigators determined a braking failure and a drunkard at the helm to be the cause. A man remiss in his duties cost the lives of everyone on board as bodies lay scattered around the tracks in various stages of mutilation. It was not a sight for the weak as the macabre vignette displayed bodies pinned under monstrously heavy train cars, limbs torn asunder, and heads severed.

As Shadow Cove mourns the event and wonders how such a tragedy could have befallen them, the Trans-Pacific Rail delegates arrive in their newly minted auto-carriages fresh out of Ford's factories to investigate what is surely a crime against man.

My eyes cross the more I read, but the more I read, the more compelled I am to learn more. Of all the things Mina has hanging on her walls, why this old article about a grisly train crash? My parents always told me my curiosity was unbecoming. Only difficult women ask questions. I've long since learned not to ask why. Except the itch of it grows with each word I read. I came here to turn my mind off and stare into the waves. Yet the itch nudges my curiosity in a decidedly delicious way, making the urge to scratch almost impossible to resist. Despite this being a clear piece of Shadow Cove history, it's a hell of a piece of memorabilia to have hanging up for all to see. Perhaps this says something about Mina. With that thought, the itch grows and I resolve to scratch it.

When I find my way to the kitchen, there's a note taped to the Kurig machine detailing the food Mina stocked in the refrigerator, what restaurants in town are good, and welcoming me to her establishment once again with a subtle reminder to stay out of locked rooms. I huff reading the reminder while the curious itch grows stronger.

Really, she said not to go in *locked* rooms. I can abide that. What she didn't say was I can't explore the house. I set the Kurig to brew a cup while I grab a parfait out of the fridge and toast a bagel. I aimlessly flip through a magazine while I eat before I pull up Shadow Cove on my map app to see just how accessible the town is from here. I still only have a single, flickering bar of service, but it holds long enough for me to get my bearings.

Despite how infinite the walk from Aiden's car to the gate felt, it was really only a couple hundred yards. Downtown Shadow Cove is roughly a mile from here, and the town itself, including the boardwalk, is a dense area where cars don't seem to be a necessity. After my day of travel, walking will do me good.

I finish my breakfast, strap on my cross-body bag, and head out the door. Mina didn't mention anything about locking up the inn, and my key is only to my room. I close the front door behind me and open it again to make sure it doesn't lock. The last thing I want is to be stuck outside until Mina arrives tonight, whenever that will be.

It's when I get to the gate that I realize no little red dot stares at me from the speaker. In fact, the gate sits ajar. I wrap my fingers around the cool wrought iron and pull, the gate swinging open easily enough. I push it all the way closed, but there's no tell-tale click of a lock engaging. Sure enough, when I pull it, the gate swings wide once again.

I look over my shoulder at the house, wary of leaving it unlocked with no one around to keep an eye on it. Until I remember Aiden's behavior last night. How he wouldn't so much as drive up to the gate let alone step foot close to the house. Maybe there's an unspoken rule that Mina isn't to be messed with. Or the town is small enough everyone shows each other common decency and locking doors isn't necessary.

Either way, I slip through the gate and leave it ajar like I found it, an unfounded fear settling in my mind that it'll lock behind me and I won't be able to get back in. The gate stays put when I take my hand off of it, and I slowly step away.

The unpaved road to the house isn't nearly as terrifying in the daylight as it is at night, but the farther I wander from the house, the more the haze creeps in. The sun's orb overhead is visible but in a washed-out smudge of color that blankets everything in a muted light. The air is cool, if not a little cold. I wonder if I should have brought a sweater with me, but I figure the walk will stir my blood enough to keep me warm.

The ocean roars as it slams into the cliffs. This time I can see out over the water, the whitecaps visible through the low fog. In the dark, the expanse was infinite. Now, I see how narrow the unpaved lane is and how close the cliffs really are. All that keeps me from taking a wrong step over the edge is a thick wooden rope about thigh height strung between posts that dot the lane. Overgrowth wraps around the posts and obscures the rope, making the protection even less reassuring. Mina wasn't lying when she said someone could easily wander over the edge if the fog were thick enough.

My heart jumps as the caw and flutter of a bird rustles nearby leaves. I laugh at my own jumpiness as I continue forward. There's nothing to be afraid of. No eyes peering at me out of the dark. No screeching, howling animals. Those terrors are gone for the day.

I brush the thought away and breathe a sigh of relief when my sneakers hit pavement and some semblance of civilization. Small ocean-side cottages dot the road, weatherbeaten and worn from the sea wind. A gust ruffles my hair, sending it whipping around my head, and I do my best to tame it.

Before long, the dive bar I passed last night emerges from around a bend. No one stands in its doorway to stare at me. In fact, it appears to be closed. It's far less intimidating under the late morning sun, but not less off-putting.

Only one small window set high on the wall allows light into the mausoleum of a bar but only through the metal security bars keeping people out. Neon signs stuck to the dirty brown siding advertising beers of all types are dull in the daytime. An aged poster for a band I've never heard of is tacked to the closed door, its torn edge fluttering in the breeze.

The eyes of the man staring at me from that doorway last night haunt me now, the way they bore into me as if he could see right through me. I see his face in my mind as if he's standing right there, only feet away. I blink and keep walking, moving a little faster past it. However it, like Little Sister's, is a presence at my back I can't seem to ignore. It's a squat, unassuming building, yet I find it both repulsive and compelling.

The structures cluster closer together the nearer I get to downtown Shadow Cove. The houses are hardly feet apart. The buildings in the downtown area lean against each other as if they need each others' support to keep standing. The boardwalk itself is a stone's throw from a small neighborhood. I glance over my shoulder and get a peek of Little Sister's leering at the town through the haze from atop its cliff. Alone and away from everything. As if nothing in Shadow Cove wants to get too close. Such absurd thoughts I think as I meander through the quaint little town, but I can't help but think them.

My stomach rumbles just as the clock strikes noon, but what's open remains sparse. Mina did mention this is the off season, so it makes sense for establishments to be slower to open when there aren't many people to open for. Now that I look around—down the sidewalk I'm walking on, across the street, around the corner—I'm the only one out. An occasional bird perches on a nearby tree branch, and a lone sea lion barks into the waves. As far as people, it's just me.

An unnerving chill settles into my skin and sinks into my bones. The heat of the afternoon sun struggles through the fog. I want to be warmed by it, but it fails, it's heat just out of reach. It's not even strong enough to burn off the haze, as if the cobwebs of the town are impossible to remove.

Eventually, I find a small cafe where I am, unsurprisingly, the only patron. A tired-looking server with bags under their eyes and a drained complexion takes my order with no small talk. Before long, I'm left to eat in silence. I finish as quickly as I can and leave a hearty tip, hoping that cheers them up some, before I leave. The town seems to finally be waking up by then, and I weave my way in and out of various shops selling jewelry, candles, and beach-themed knickknacks. Typical tourist fare for the single tourist wandering the streets.

Pressure settles between my shoulder blades as I make my way to the boardwalk. The coaster car rattles up the hill before rocketing down the other side, seats vacant, the air devoid of thrilling screams. The boardwalk's promenade is empty, yet the subtle scent of fried foods and the sugary sweetness of cotton candy hangs in the air. At least that tells me last night's view of the boardwalk wasn't a hallucination. It really does open for business, if just not right now.

In the middle of the day.

On a weekend.

Waves roar on the other side of the promenade, the beach warm and inviting, but it too sits empty. I'm starting to wonder if there's something I'm missing.

The gentle tap of footsteps sound behind me. I turn to find a security guard ambling along the promenade, glancing from left to right at nothing but empty carnival rides and closed game booths. I make my way to him with what I hope is an endearing smile.

"Excuse me."

His bored expression turns on me as if I've inconvenienced him. I clear my throat and swallow the knot forming there.

"I'm just here for a vacation, and I was wondering," I motion to the emptiness around us, "where is everyone?"

The man glances around, his well-manicured mustache barely moving as he opens his mouth to speak. "People don't get going until later around here. Come back around dinner and it'll pick up."

"I see that," I say with a tight smile. "Thank you."

Helpfully unhelpful. I've heard of lazy beach towns, but this is something else. I'm not sure what I was expecting him to say, but his response leaves me unsatisfied. People must work. The residents of Shadow Cove have errands to run. Business must go on. I know it's the off season, but this seems really off.

Shadow Cove certainly moves at its own pace, and it will not be deterred otherwise.

I make my way off the boardwalk's skeletal remains, its emptiness making me anxious, and continue my wandering around town. I stumble across a local history museum nestled between a gift shop and a stationary store, both currently closed. The itch from the article on the wall at Little Sister's comes roaring back, and with little else to keep me occupied, I find my hand reaching for the door. It opens with ease instead of me being met with a locked jolt.

Inside, of course, is just as empty as out. Displays of old Shadow Cove abound, but there's no one around to see them, and no one inside to guide anyone through the local history. So, I make my own way, stopping at each station, admiring the sepia-colored pictures and reading each caption as I come to it.

Shadow Cove started as an old gold rush town, abandoned by Spanish missionaries for unknown reasons. They were long gone by the time the Forty-Niners got here. People quickly learned that while there was no gold in these hills, there was plenty of fish. From there, it turned into a port. When wealthier people started making trips on the new railways, it became a vacation destination for long distance and local tourists alike.

The history of Shadow Cove is otherwise unremarkable until I come across the same article about the train crash I saw earlier at the inn. The display has that article plus a handful more, a railroad spike, and a woman's hat still dirtied by coal dust and dented from impact.

If this crash has a place in a local history museum, then it must have had an impact on the town. That could explain why Mina has it framed on her wall, however morbid that may be. Having dozens of people die on one's doorstep tends to leave a mark. Another article says thirty-seven bodies were recovered. The passenger manifest showed that one never was. Thrown from the wreck, perhaps. The tracks were close enough to the cliffside when they were still there. No surprise the residents voted to pull up the tracks after the accident and forced the rail line to reroute.

Such a decision cut off tourism to the area for a number of years until paved roads and more prolific electricity was able to make its way here. By then the damage had been done.

"Do you have any questions? I know it's a lot of information."

I jump at the voice, my heart in my throat as I spin round to find an older gentleman shuffling his way to me. Wisps of gray hair coat his head, and tiny spectacles perch on the tip of his nose.

"You scared me. I didn't see you there," I tell him, breathless, but trying to keep my voice light. The last thing I want to do is chastise him.

"How long you here for?" he asks, ignoring my exclamation as if I said nothing at all.

"The week," I tell him. "I'm staying up at Little Sister's. I guess I didn't realize how off the off season was," I add with a light chuckle, but his face remains impassive.

"Folks in this town get a late start, some of them anyway," he says as he looks past me to the display at my back. "Hopefully, you won't get drawn into their habits." I frown, but he motions around the small space. "Yell if you need anything."

Without another word, he turns around and shuffles away from me, through a door and out of sight. People are strange in Shadow Cove. Part of me wants to go back to the hotel, unnerved as I am by the empty town. The inn is safe, known, with a locking door. But the history of Shadow Cove draws me back in, the display of the train crash like an anchor on my psyche. I finish reading before moving onto the next display, equally as macabre. I guess for someplace like Shadow Cove, things like this are going to be news.

A picture of a familiar house catches my eye. Little Sister's takes up the frame, the photo from only a couple years after the train crash. Three portraits are positioned next to it, the dour faces of an older man and woman, and the soft, inviting gaze of a young man, likely younger than me at the time. Something swirls in my chest when I glance at his face. Something familiar yet chilling, like a nail scraping down the back of my neck. The headline is just as catching:

$$\cdot \quad \cdot \quad \cdot$$

GRAY SKY INN SITS ABANDONED AFTER GRISLY MURDERS OF PROPRIETORS

A refuge to all and sundry who need a place to rest their heads and a hearty meal to warm their bellies, the Gray Sky Inn will host no more. In the early hours of the morning, unbeknownst to the tenants dreaming in their rooms, Mr. and Mrs. Pennington were brutally murdered, their bodies left in the cellar of the house to be found by the cook the following morning. Their son, Nathaniel Pennington, hasn't been seen since the previous evening. Authorities are searching for his whereabouts, but hope dwindles by the day. The condition of the bodies are such that no human could possibly imitate, their innards freed from the confines of their flesh and their veins emptied of all their blood. For only a monster could do something so monstrous.

Far more florid than the article about the train crash, it's no surprise a story such as that warrants the whimsical words of storytelling. Even then sensational spinning sold papers. While such a thing happening in the same place where they sleep would deter some people, my morbid curiosity is piqued even more. So much for no work on my vacation. Only I don't see this as work. I thought I needed calm. A beach. Maybe a lurid book to read. *This* is what I need. A distraction. Something to keep my mind occupied, not empty.

With a house as old as Shadow Cove itself, it's no surprise it's bore witness to all the events that befell the town.

I want to pluck those memories from its bones.

With the details of Shadow Cove's history firmly planted in my mind, I make my way back to the inn, my nerves buzzing with something like excitement.

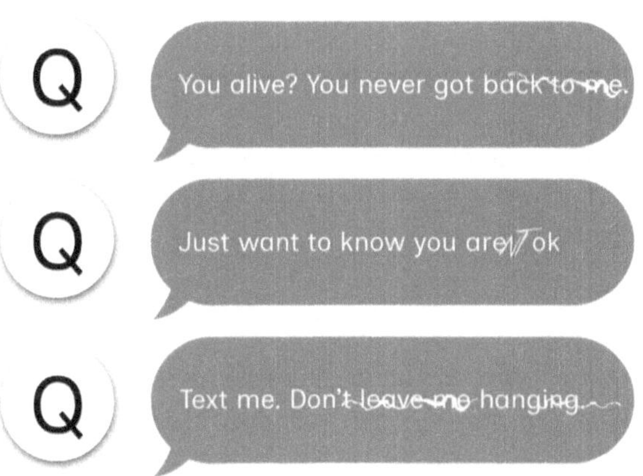

Q
You alive? You never got back to me.
Q
Just want to know you aren't ok
Q
Text me. Don't leave me hanging.

4

I start on the first floor and work my way up, trying knobs and handles that may allow me peeks of the secrets of Little Sister's, the old Gray Sky Inn, that aren't otherwise obvious. Unfortunately, my search is proving to be disappointingly mundane. What doors aren't locked are closets, a laundry room, and an overflow pantry.

There is one door on the first floor that stops me in my tracks, sunlight glinting off of a shiny new padlock barring access. The wood is old, and instead of a knob there's an old lifting latch that does nothing more than clink when I touch it. That padlock keeps the door firmly in place. I can't help but wonder if this door leads to the basement and the scene of a crime more than a hundred years old.

The itch at the back of my head grows incessant, the feeling more like an abrasion than a tickle. Without trying my hand at lock picking, this door is off limits to me.

I grab a fruit cup from the fridge before making my way upstairs, pausing at the frames on the wall to re-read the article that started this snipe hunt. I eat as I read, trying to find hidden meaning where there is none. Before long I move onto other frames. Old pictures of people long dead, but one gives me pause. A young man, handsome in his portrait, with soft features and light hair. I know this face, but from where keeps slipping my mind. It's something recent. I can taste it.

I pull my phone from my back pocket and do a reverse image search, hoping it pulls something up, but my service is suspect. I switch over to the Wi-Fi, but it must be on the fritz. The signal is too low to use.

I stuff my phone back into my pocket. "Fuck."

It's going to bug the hell out of me until I can figure out where I know his face from. Using my laptop is out of the question until I can ask Mina about the internet. Quinn must be losing her mind. I shoot off a quick text to her and hope it stumbles its way through the poor connection. I haven't heard from her since I got here. She must be busy with work, and she knows I'm here decompressing. I'm sure everything is fine.

My investigation brings me to the second floor landing, my room just to my right, and a shadowed hallway to my left. I place the empty cup on a nearby table, reminding myself to grab it when I'm done, and step lightly down the darkened hall. Dust hangs heavier in the air here than it does on my side of the landing. I brush a finger along a piece of wainscoting and leave behind a cleared trail among dust, my fingertip coming up gray. Closed doors line the hallway. Shadows absorb the rain of dust I brush off my fingers before I wrap my hand around a knob and push. Nothing. The door is locked.

I make my way down the hall, stepping lightly and quietly testing each door even though I know I'm the only one in the inn.

I'm *pretty sure* I'm the only one in the inn.

A wooden creak shatters the quiet, and I gasp. My hand

knocks against the door knob I was about to grab, and I turn to face the greater hallway. I'm at the end. Dirty, dead flowers in a ceramic vase sit atop a table coated with dust. Only instead of laying hidden under a blanket of darkness, muted light slices into the hall from the door opposite.

A door that was closed not seconds before.

I glance down the hall, toward the light, but there's no one there.

"Hello?"

My voice sounds tiny and stunted in the narrow hall. No one responds. I step closer to the now-open room and get my first glimpse inside.

What I thought was another guest room is actually an office. Not as grand as the house but still adorned with a heavy wooden desk and bookshelves lining at least one wall. A faded Persian rug blankets the center of the room, and two chairs sit facing each other in front of a cold fireplace.

Mina's words spring to the front of my mind, to respect locked doors. Except this door isn't locked. I reach for the knob and test the mechanism. Clearly unlocked, not broken or not shut all the way as if it's a room I'm not meant to see.

I step to the doorway. The door creaks again, and I push it open. Something in my periphery draws my attention. When I look, a stone drops into my stomach. Like the mark I left in the dust on the woodwork at the beginning of the hall, four streaks smear over the door jamb into the room. As if someone gripped the wood and dragged their fingers through the dust before entering.

Images from last night surface. Something in the hall. This hall. This room. I glance at the streaks again before peeking through the crack to glimpse behind the door, bracing myself to find eyes staring back at me. It's only bookshelves. I push the door open wider and step inside to find a room with no real place to hide. At least, nowhere to hide that's visible. In a house like this, secret passages aren't out of the question. The thought frays my nerves, and I try to push the feeling aside, not wanting to think about who could have access to my room without me knowing it.

The room, like the hall, is coated in a fine layer of dust. The shelves, books, and old spectacles on the desk are all dulled by it. Which means if I touch anything it'll be obvious someone was in here. While the door is unlocked, I don't need to advertise that I was snooping in Mina's house.

It's a spartan office, yet the afternoon sun beaming through the window adds a cozy element to it all. The books lining the shelves are about nature, business, and global politics. Nothing that piques my interest. A dust-coated lantern sits at the corner of the desk with a closed book next to it. I lean over the chair to peek at the title, only to find none. With a fingernail, I lift the cover to find it's a book on the indigenous tribes of the Philippines. Accurate and not at all bigoted, I'm sure.

My fingers graze the stylized knobs of a drawer in the desk before they wrap around one and tug. An old accounting ledger sits inside with comparably less dust than the rest of the room but enough to show my guilt. So I leave it alone and move to the next drawer. It isn't until I get to the bottom, the largest drawer of all, that I find anything of interest.

A whiff of old paper hits my nose when I open it. The past stares back with long-dead eyes in newsprint black. Old newspapers and a short stack of leather-bound albums sit in the desk drawer. All of them are blissfully dust free. I stack the newspapers gently on the floor next to the drawer and find the albums are photo albums. The gilded letters look hand drawn. I run my finger along the letters, and the itch at the back of my mind turns into a poke.

I pull the album from the drawer and sit on the floor next

to the desk before placing the book in my lap. Inside are images of open land, the ocean in the background. A ground-breaking. The frame of a building. Slowly, the pieces fall into place the more pages I turn, and Little Sister's, or rather, Gray Sky, takes shape. The original proprietors sit solemnly on the steps of the front porch, a husband and wife with what I assume is an adult son.

Then it clicks, where I know the face on the wall down-stairs. It's the same face from the display at the historical soci-ety. The same face that looks at me here. Nathaniel, adult son who went missing after the brutal murders of his parents. The pictures aren't many, but there are enough to tell me the orig-inal proprietors were proud of this inn only to have it ripped away from them.

I pull out another album, this one black and etched in red foil. It looks newer, held together better than the aging photo album I just handled. Inside are a variety of destinations. The Parthenon in Greece. The Colosseum in Rome. The Hagia Sofia in Istanbul. A market in Delhi. All scenes with no single person as a focal point. Crowds. Places. Until I turn the page and find the portraits.

Mina.

Sitting still and ramrod straight, she stares into the soul of the camera. Her dress has a high collar and stiff shoulders. It's something out of the past. There are no dates on them, and I can't help but wonder if they're those carnival photos someone can get where they dress in antique clothes and pose for a fee. They're all pasted to the pages, so I'm not going to pry them up. If they are new and meant to look old, whoever did it did a great job aging them. They look authentic.

I'd believe they were if I didn't know Mina as a real live person I spoke with last night. This is a relative, maybe. That's a rational explanation. But the more pages I turn, the less rational it feels.

Especially when I get to the last page, and my heart stops. Mina and the adult son of the original proprietors together in a photo.

He looks nearly the same from his family portrait to this one despite the change in clothing style. He sits in a chair with his hands on his lap while Mina stands next to him, her hand on his shoulder. Their pose is meant to evoke a sense of authority. The man with the dutiful woman at his side. But their faces, the way Mina gazes unflinchingly into the camera, tells me it's the opposite. There's a subtle upward turn of her mouth and a gleam in her eye that shines despite the matte paper the photo is printed on.

I shake my head when I realize I called her Mina. It might as well be Mina's twin, but I know that's not possible. What is possible is the young man killed his parents and ran off with Mina's ancestor. Without the use of photo editing software, what other explanation is there?

My fingers brush along the delicate picture board, grazing both of their faces. The lines of him are harsher, as if he aged some, but not much. The look in his eye is sharper, more discerning. Knowing. Mina's is all mischief and mayhem, daring the onlooker to question what's occurring right in front of them, whatever that happens to be.

The album slams closed with a resounding thud, and I pull another from the drawer. This one even newer, the pages with plastic protective sheets and designs out of the seventies. Something tells me not to open it. Put everything back and walk away now. Except the itch is strong, and before my mind can knock some sense into my limbs, my fingers grab the cover and turn the page.

At first, I don't comprehend what I'm seeing. There's no

sense to be found on the pages. As I turn page after page and the pictures move through the decades, disbelief turns to confusion. Right behind it is fear, slow and seeping through the cracks of me.

Mina is in many of them, her styles changing by the page. Corseted Edwardian to drop-waisted flapper to a forties pinup. And on and on. The same man from the last album is with her, a near-constant presence on her arm or in the background. Come the fifties, another face starts appearing, one I know was staring at me from the doorway of the dive bar at the end of the unpaved lane. The seventies brings my CRG driver, Aiden, looking exactly the same as I saw him, yet time requiring him to be fifty years older.

I don't understand what I'm seeing.

The eighties has Owen, his soft features and youthful look seemingly eternal. They flit in and out of the photos, in and out of scenes. Every once in a while there's a landscape, a monument of some kind denoting where they might be, but I don't recognize any of them. They could be anywhere or nowhere.

It takes me a second to pick up the pattern, but when I do, I flip back through the pages to check my work, my thoughts spiraling into chaos. If the pictures of this motley crew aren't taken indoors, they're taken outside, but only at night. Not a single picture taken outdoors is during the day.

My brain sputters, the thoughts making no sense. Shadow Cove is a small town. Very small. Aiden said they all knew each other. He said he knew Mina. Owen obviously knows Mina. Maybe they're just close friends who like Halloween. Playing dress up. Shadow Cove doesn't seem to offer much in the entertainment department.

A door slams and Mina's lilting voice calls through the house. I jolt, panic racing through me as I fumble with my phone and see hours have passed when it only felt like minutes. My head spins as I try to make sense of my lost time. Perhaps it's guilt at rooting through this desk I have no business looking through.

I scramble to put everything away, closing the drawer as quietly as I can, and tiptoe out of the office. Since the door was closed before, I close it again even though I wasn't the one who opened it. I don't want to draw Mina's attention to this room. She doesn't need any ideas that I've been snooping. I try to comport myself, put on a happier face, and push the thoughts from my mind before I venture out to see her. Only everything is in knots. I don't know what I just found, but I'm going to need some distance from it in order to process it. It's too wild. Too unruly.

Perhaps I'll go to the dive bar for a drink and use their Wi-Fi. See if I can get a better connection off property. When I make my way to the common areas, Mina is already buzzing, excitedly putting together dinner. She is a flame flitting around the kitchen as she grabs ingredients and tools, and I'm a moth helplessly drawn to her.

I see the knife in my hand before I feel the wood of its handle. I've already cut half a pepper before I realize I grabbed it to begin with. When she sees me trying to help, Mina tries to shoo me away, but I insist, my voice a great distance from my mind. The more she chatters, the more at ease I get, the silly thoughts from before, the information I found, fading to mist.

Distance. I need distance from it. Tomorrow, I'll go to the bar when it opens. A drink to clear my head should help. Maybe then I'll find something that'll give me reasonable answers to the questions I have. There has to be a rational explanation for what I saw, and I will find it.

Owen makes an appearance and begins work on another

light fixture. We lock eyes as I rub seasoning into a cut of steak. He has deceptively innocent eyes, rounded features, and muscular arms. He certainly looks like the same person from those photos. A person who should be decades older than he is.

Mina brings me back to her attention with a question, and I answer as light-heartedly as I can. Out of the corner of my eye I watch a smile curl up the corner of Owen's mouth—devious and telling—before he turns back to his work. Mina places a hand over mine and lightly presses her warmth into my chilled flesh.

"I hope you're enjoying your stay so far," she says with a smile, her gaze boring into my soul.

As if she sees. As if she knows what I know, but can't possibly.

"I am," I tell her, smiling back, and mean it.

With each word out of her mouth, the heat of her touch, her soft gaze, my worries melt away. My parents' untimely death is a burden lifted from my shoulders, as if the distraction of her voice makes me feel weightless. Unburdened. Finally.

I have a hard time holding onto the images I found. The connections I'm making that can't possibly connect. Mina laughs, and it's a cozy blanket around my shoulders drawing me to her. Her presence, the nearness of her body, makes it hard for me to focus on anything but her. My hand holds tightly to the knife as I chop.

From the corner of my eye, Mina pulls her hand from the bowl of raw beef, blood coating her fingers. She runs her tongue along one digit before pressing it into her mouth and sucking it clean.

I inhale a shuddering breath and turn to her only to find both her hands submerged in the bowl as she tosses the raw cubes with seasoning and sauce. She keeps talking as if that moment didn't happen. As if nothing interrupted her sentence at all.

Mina's voice is a balm as it washes over me, much like the blood coating her hand. Her licking it from her fingers that I didn't see. I blink hard, hiding my feelings behind me slicing through an onion's heart and releasing its tear-inducing smell.

It's been a long day. A long couple of days. Perhaps I wore myself out more than I expected to. Certainly not a relaxing start to a vacation. The more Mina talks, the more she brushes against me as we work, the lighter my shoulders get. The calmer my thoughts get. Soon enough all I can think about is Mina and this delicious meal we're preparing together.

5

"Be careful," Mina says, as I make my way out the door. "The cliff's edge is closer than you think. And the animals are hungry."

A reminder.

A warning.

Respect the night.

"Of course," I tell her with a tight smile. "I won't be out all night."

After the gate is at my back, I realize I have no idea why I said anything at all. She's not my dorm mother. I'm renting a room from her, and I'm a grown woman. I've lived in this world for long enough to know how it works. I may not be a wilderness expert, but I'm not stupid. As much as I appreciate her reminder, I can't help but feel condescended to. It's a familiar feeling. One I've had most of my life as people—my parents more often than not—spoke to me like every day was my first day out in the world.

I'm sure Mina has the best of intentions, but the road to hell is paved with them.

This time I'm more prepared for the dark and the perpetual fog that coats this seaside world. I have my phone out, the light on bright despite the streetlights that line the lane. I walk with purpose over the rutted dirt road, my laptop bag slapping at my leg as I march. I try not to give those shining lamps too much thought. After the ride in with Aiden coupled with a day of travel, my head was a mess. Our conversations on the ride didn't help. It's not like Mina ran out after I checked in and set the lights back out as part of some elaborate ruse to muddle my head. What matters is they're there now and are helping to push back the claustrophobic night.

A screech rips through the quiet. I yelp in return, an involuntary noise. My heart races, and I struggle to get its pattering under control. I keep walking, hoping the rhythm will help to slow my thundering heart. Each step is purposeful and controlled despite my instincts telling me to move faster.

It's just an animal, Lucy. You're bigger than it. You're fine.

Somewhat comforting are the glittering lights of the boardwalk in the distance, nestled on the far side of the churning waves. The muffled screams of riders on the rollercoaster float over the inlet and wrap around me in a gentle squeeze, telling me there really are people here. I am not alone despite how alone I convince myself I want to be. How alone I feel up here on the cliffs.

As the dive bar grows closer, its squat cement structure a stump in the surrounding shadows, I expect to hear loud music thumping through its open door. Instead, all is strangely quiet except for low shuffling from within.

I slow my pace, as if afraid I'm going to spook something, but there's nothing to spook. The door is open, the light inside on, and the neon tacked to the outside walls hums a lulling drone.

As I walk through the door I expect a record scratch, the

world of the bar to come to a screeching halt as the outsider steps into their midst. Perhaps I've seen too many movies, or I'm far too uncomfortable in my own skin at the moment. The only person who glances my way is the bartender who nods as he continues to stock his garnishes.

Garnishes. Because the inside is nothing like the outside. Starting with maraschino cherries, lime and lemon wedges, and olives. A full suite of liquor sits on shelves against the mirror at the back of the bar, most of it of middling quality. No plastic handles of vodka that might as well have been made in a toilet bowl. The taps include old classics and local crafts. Today's beer special is an IPA I've never heard of, and the seasonal drink is called a Foggy Night. How appropriate. It's a vodka martini flavored with bergamot and lavender and topped with swirling mist.

From the outside, this is not the kind of drink I would expect from this place. My thoughts don't change from the inside. It's not the dingy, dirty hole it looks like from the street, but it's not an upscale lounge either. Booths dotted with their own banker's lamps line one wall while small round tables and chairs lay scattered around the room. Worn stools line an equally worn bar, and a pool table takes up a corner. A couple of people reset the table and talk amongst themselves.

I order a Foggy Night, figuring what the hell, and a glass of water. Heat flames my cheeks when he hands me a purple drink so dark it's nearly black overflowing with mist, looking more like a witch's cauldron than something I should consume. I pay and shuffle my way to a back booth, out of the way and tucked into a dark corner. I don't want to be noticed, although until my drink stops hemorrhaging mist, I might as well have a trail leading right to me.

As I'm pulling my laptop from my bag, before I can turn it on and connect to the bar's Wi-Fi, someone slides into the booth in front of me. Someone I didn't see coming despite my clear view of the front door. Someone who didn't make noise until his body scraped against the cushioned seating. Someone with a piercing gaze that nails me in place.

He offers me only a smirk as he rests a bottle on the table and clasps his hands in front of him. He's wearing black, a black t-shirt with a small hole in the collar, black jacket with a popped collar, and hair a color blond that doesn't exist in nature. Dark roots peek through the moon-light-blond strands as he runs a hand through his hair, a silver ring on his middle finger. He's more intimidating up close than when I first saw him driving past in Aiden's car the other night.

"I was wondering when you'd make your way here," he says, his voice raspy and deep.

It sends shudders through me, fear and desire coiling deep in my gut, battling with the last shreds of feminism I'm desperately clinging to.

I clear my throat while holding his disconcerting gaze. "As you can see, this table is already taken. Please go sit some-where else."

My finger presses into the power button on my laptop. The subtle bong of it booting is the punctuation at the end of my sentence.

He doesn't move. His hands stay clasped, and a smile pulls his lips across his angular jaw. The barest hint of a shadow touches his cheeks. "It's been a while since Mina had a guest. Good to see she hasn't gotten rusty."

His eyes travel down my body, what isn't hidden under the table, before making their way back to my face. I keep my look stoic—stone—my gaze immovable despite the war being waged inside of me. I could dive into his piercing blue eyes. His rugged handsomeness is undeniable. Unfortunately, his uninvited intrusion into my evening overrides most of those feelings.

I place my fingers on the keyboard and start typing, trying to do what I came here to do. Research Little Sister's. "I won't say it again." I glance at him over the top of the laptop screen before diverting my attention back to my search results.

"Is she making you comfortable? I hope she is," he says, continuing to ignore what I'm saying.

Instead of speaking again, because clearly that isn't working, I lock my screen and make to slide from the booth only to jump back as he kicks his booted foot next to me, blocking me in. A round-toed black boot dusted in dirt connected to a leg clad in black denim sits hardly an inch from me. I look at him with a scowl.

"Let me out," I say through gritted teeth, my annoyance mingling with thoughts that should not be crossing my mind. Also fear. Just a hint of it.

"Getting out isn't what you want," he says before he takes a sip of his beer. "Is it?"

I seethe, anger overpowering whatever other emotions I may be contending with. "I just said—"

A sharp inhale escapes me as his other booted foot snaps against the bench, this time between my legs. A matching boot nestles at my apex, my thighs framing it as he continues to smile at me. He has me boxed in, making climbing out even harder.

"You came here. You found us." He *tsks* as he shakes his head. "No. You don't want to get out. You're desperate to get *in*."

"Who the fuck are you?" I spit, my rage oozing out of me like the mist from my drink.

Yet right behind it is curiosity, a lingering pulse of fear, and a heady throb of desire. Without me noticing, his outside foot now presses against my thigh, pushing my legs together around his other boot.

He points at my laptop. "You won't find what you're looking for in there." He points to the wall on the other side of the small lamp casting a dull yellow haze across the table. "Everything you need is in that house. Everything you *want*."

"Leave me alone," I whisper, my voice choked and weak.

I dig my feet into the ground to try and get some leverage, but my shoes slip, and I thump into the boot between my legs, my thighs squeezing him. He presses into me like a pedal, and my breath catches.

My hand jerks to his boot in a feeble attempt to push it away, but my body betrays me. He grinds his boot between my legs, the pressure salacious and sinful as it mixes with the danger of the situation. Instead of pushing him away, my hand merely rests atop his boot.

Images invade my mind. They flash across my vision like a projector, replacing the smug face sitting sentinel in front of me. Images of the man dragging his thumb along my lip dance in front of my eyes, flickering over the real version sitting across from me. I can practically feel it, the salty sweet taste of him. My tongue licks the dryness of my lips away as I look toward the bar, anxious for help that isn't there. The room is empty. The lights are dim. There's no one here but the two of us in this booth.

Images of hands roaming my body, along my waist, over my stomach, across my breasts float through my mind. Only they're not just thoughts. His hands remain clasped on the table, but as sure as I feel my clothes on my skin, hands slide across my body. There's nothing there, but I feel each finger. Each pinch. Each twist. Each press.

"I don't think you want me to," he says, his voice a haze wrapping around me. "Do you, Lucy?"

"How—how—"

I can't get the words out. Phantom hands prowl my body. Slide under my bra, down my pants, probe at my opening. There are no hands to be seen. Not even a breeze to ruffle my shirt, but my skin sings with the touch of ghosts.

He smirks as he leans forward. I lean in to meet him, as if we're attached and resisting isn't an option. He presses my laptop closed and reaches for my neck. His fingers wrap around my flaming flesh, his chilled touch a relief to the heat swarming me.

Fear presses at my skin, desperate to get out. To escape whatever sorcery this is. Only weakness is right behind it, pulsing a desire to lay myself out on this table and let this man do with me what he will. I don't even know his name, but that, of all things, seems irrelevant right now.

He remains silent. Instead, he pulls me closer to him by my neck. I lift off my seat, my ass hovering over the cushion. It's just enough to grind me into the toe of his boot. His free hand grabs my jaw, his thumb pressing under my chin while his fingers slide over my tongue and halfway down my throat.

"You're nearly there," he whispers, as he probes my mouth, his fingers sliding along my teeth, his nails grazing the back of my throat.

My eyes water as my tongue reaches out to take his hand. I'm rooted to the table, barely hanging on, until my hand snaps out and grabs his wrist. I hold him steady, four fingers deep into my mouth as I wrap my lips around him, resting my teeth against his flesh.

"Yes," he whispers, his eyes hooded. "Do it. You're so close."

Close to what, my brain can't comprehend. An orgasm? He's not wrong as the hands keep molesting my body, my mind having a hard time tuning them out. I'm repulsed yet turned on. It's a war inside of me, and I'm not sure which side will win.

Then an urge comes over me.

To bite.

I press my teeth harder into his fingers, the salty tang of his flesh sharp on my tongue. The bar is dark, the only light the dim glow of the table lamp. My drink has stopped spewing mist, and I press my teeth a little harder into this strange man's flesh.

His mouth parts. He watches me with such intent, such desire. I can't see past the table, can't see anything below his waist, but I wonder. Imagine.

I bite harder.

Salt turns to metal as blood pools in my mouth, slicking over my tongue and welling in my jaw. Teeth grind against bone as I keep biting, forcing my way through his fingers.

"Do it," he mutters again, as his hand disappears under the table before his arm starts moving at a steady beat.

Bones crunch as my teeth break through flesh and bone. With each splinter my fear ebbs, replaced by control. My lip twitches into a sneer for a moment before I clench one more time and bite clean through his fingers. Bone grinds against bone. Flesh squelches and rips as I tear them from his hand. The tip-tap of blood hits the table from the rivulets flowing down my chin. His fingers cluster in my mouth, their flesh thick and gamey.

Laughter erupts around me, as if it's coming out of the walls. The man's jaw hangs open as he guffaws into the empty bar, a hearty belly laugh as he watches me. He holds up his hand to show his fingers missing at each big knuckle. Blood sloshes around my mouth as I grind through the digits. Spitting them out never crosses my mind. Perhaps if I can consume a piece of him, chew him up and swallow him, he'll know the control I have. Over myself and over him.

I have defeated him. Broken him. Destroyed him.

Only when I blink and see his hand whole, yet my mouth remains full, my resolve, my confidence, falters. The man only laughs harder. I must have a look on my face. Horror. Terror. Disgust. Before I can form the words, his face goes deadly.

"Swallow."

I hit the back of the booth, as if the man shoved me, but he remains still. A phantom hand wraps around my throat and tilts my face up. Whatever is in my mouth slides down my throat in thick globs. My eyes water as chewed flesh drops into my body piece by piece, inching along my esophagus to splash into the core of me. Meaty and bloody, they're poison with a hint of sweetness. My veins ignite with it, this stranger's curse, as my body absorbs him.

This demon.

"So close," he says with another smile before he slides out of the booth.

He leaves me coated in blood, pieces of him worming their way through my body, and on the verge of both orgasm and destructive rage.

"Did you want another?"

The voice is such a jarring intrusion I gasp and look up only to find the bartender standing at the edge of the table. The low thrum of music filters back into my consciousness as the blue light from my laptop screen casts a cold glow over my heaving chest. I tap my chin only to find it dry. No sticky residue.

He points at my drink, at the empty glass that held the drink I don't remember consuming and looks at me again.

"No," I choke, then shake my head. "One's enough for me."

He shrugs and walks away as I scan the bar. The same handful of people remain scattered about with their drinks. The same pair are still at the billiard table in the corner, balls clacking as they play their game. No blond man dressed in black who just fed me his flesh. As I gather my things and stand, there's not even a dent in the bench cushion across from me. As if he wasn't there at all.

My heart thunders, panic welling inside me. A buzz runs through my veins. What the fuck just happened? *Did I hallucinate all that?* Never have I ever seen anything like what I just witnessed. Not in my dreams or daydreams or even my nightmares. That man is nowhere to be found. I hustle out the door and glance over my shoulder as I make my way to the unpaved road. The lit end of a cigarette flares in the darkness, but I can't see anything else. No fingers on the cigarette. No face behind the light.

Laughter, sounding a lot like a crow's caw, ripples through the night. I pick up my pace, desperate to get back to the safety of Little Sister's.

L
Service sucks. Not sure this will make it out. But I'm here, relaxing. Please don't worry.

6

—————

Falling asleep is a chore as I think about my encounter with the man at the bar. A man whose name I don't know. Who injected something into my head, into my body. It slithers through my veins, buzzing beneath my skin as I lie here. It's an electric pulse that keeps my heart thundering, anxiety and nerves battling with each other.

All the stress I've bottled up, from my tightly controlled life to my parents' deaths, must finally be coming to a head. I hallucinated biting off a man's fingers and eating them, for fuck's sake. The ship has sailed on normal.

Eventually, I settle into a restless sleep that has me hovering somewhere between oblivion and wakefulness. Time slips, and when I wake again it's the middle of the night. A black night sky paints the windows on the balcony door, and the air in my room is still.

Too still.

Hunger rumbles my stomach. I try to ignore it, but the growling turns into a raucous snarl that pulls me from the bed. I don't worry about my flimsy nightgown, unafraid what

Mina will say if she sees me in it. Part of me wonders what she would think if she saw me like this, if she would like what she saw. I shake the notion away. They're late night thoughts not meant to see the light of day.

I place my hand on the knob and turn.

Nothing.

I try again, this time jerking harder. I watch the door as I pull, but it doesn't move in the frame.

Stuck, maybe.

The lock on the knob is engaged and stays put when I try to turn it. Which means it's locked from the outside.

Mina has locked me in overnight.

A million thoughts rush through my head. Does she not trust me? Is it for my safety? For hers? What if there's a fire?

Lucy.

A shiver strokes the shell of my ear as phantom lips brush against the skin. It's a whisper, but the words are clear. As if whoever said it stands right next to me.

Chills prickle my skin as I turn toward the voice, only to find an empty room. At least I think it's empty. Ambient light filters through the sheer curtains, and I find the outlines of the bed, a dresser, the TV. I stand as still as I can. Waiting. Nothing moves. Nothing breathes except me.

Perhaps I'm closer to sleep than I am awake after all. Maybe this is all a dream.

Lucy.

Another whisper at my ear, and my eyes flutter. Like a hook in my center, I'm pulled toward the balcony. My hands rest on the door handles, and the doors swing open with a gentle pull. Ocean air washes over me, the roar of the waves in the distance a calming lull. I wrap my hands around the iron railing and let the moon's light wash over me as I watch the fog crawl across the property. It slithers through the grass like a snake, seeking something out. Like it's alive.

Something yips, then screeches, shattering the serenity. Panic rises under my skin, swirling with the alien feeling of *something* slithering just underneath. Something the man from the bar put in me. Something I took from him willingly.

A spark flashes in the dark yard, followed by a glowing ember. It casts a subtle light on lips wrapped around a cigarette. I gasp, shove myself away from the railing, and slam the balcony doors closed, not caring if Mina hears me. I throw the lock and scramble back into bed, my feet barely grazing the floor. As if there's something waiting under the bed to pounce the first chance it gets.

In this moment, I'm actually grateful for the exterior lock on my door. Unless he can fly, that man can't get in.

Despite my thundering heart, I rest my head against the pillow and the room fades. My flesh settles against my bones, the essence of that man invading each atom. I'm too tired to fight it. Too tired to will it away. Besides, it feels more like a comfort than a cancer. Sleep lingers in my periphery, hanging just out of reach.

Time passes in an incoherent blur as I doze, but I'm aware of the room. The bed pressing against my body. The blanket spread atop me. My body and the weight of it, but only insofar as it exists. I lift my hand to scratch an itch, but nothing moves. I try again, but no matter how much I will it, my body remains unresponsive.

Even as I feel something slither up my leg—a cool hand made of mist, fingers pressing into my hot flesh—I can't move. I turn my head, the only thing I seem able to do, but find nothing but my room coated in a filmy haze. My eyes desperately try to focus, but no matter how hard I blink the world remains blurry. I can't tell if I'm awake or asleep. Is this a dream or some warped reality?

Another hand roams up my other leg, sliding along my skin until it reaches my bare apex, exposed for the phantom caressing me.

"Please . . ." I manage to mutter, but my mouth stops working before I can get to *stop*.

It sounds like pleading to my ears. Begging. My mind wants it to be anything but, but my body responds to the touch against my will. My veins pulse with need, responding to the phantom. As the ghostly hands caress my flesh, pieces of *him*, the man from the bar, answer the touch from within. Each brush, each stroke, I feel it inside and out. It's invasive and intoxicating.

Hands spread my legs, and they move without resistance. I couldn't resist if I tried. I'm not convinced I would. Something probes me, chilled to the touch but firm. In and out. In and out. It moves to my ass, slithering between my cheeks before it presses at my tight hole, meeting resistance before forcing its way in. I gasp at the pierce of pressure and welcome the intrusion. My body is laid bare for the phantom's taking.

Movement draws my blurry gaze to the silhouette of someone in the room with me. It's not *him*, but the familiarity of the body calls to me. Pale moonlight outlines his soft hair and narrow shoulders. I don't need to see his face to know it's Nathaniel, the original proprietors' son, haunting my mind. He stays well out of reach while the probing intensifies. I can't help but wonder if the two are the same.

Something slides up my hip, under my nightgown and across my stomach before wrapping around one breast, then the other. It feels like the bar, like the hands that man let loose on me finally have access to my body they didn't before while *he* molests me from within. And Nathaniel . . . Nathaniel . . .

What I can only describe as a tongue, broad and wet, laps against my folds, over my clit, and my nipples pebble with pleasure. The phantom wraps around them, squeezing them tighter, twisting my nipples until I cry out in pain. Dampness slicks my thighs, and my pussy gets another lick for my effort.

The phantom enters me, filling me from in front and behind, spreading my legs as wide as they'll go. Phantom fingers run along my body, up my chest, until they wrap around my throat and squeeze.

Images flash through my mind: the man from the bar, long-dead Nathaniel, and Mina. Their faces blur in a swirl of flesh and hair as I imagine their hands and their mouths traveling across my body. The phantom pumps into me, the weight of it pressing against my body as it fills me. Its hands hold me in place, flick and twist and choke as it fucks me. Moans clog my throat until it squeezes even that out of me.

There is no bucking. No reaching out. There is nothing to grab onto. I am immobile and completely at this phantom's whims. The little voice at the back of my mind tells me to fight while I give myself to this thing about to fuck me to death. The fight battling in my mind fizzles, easing into a hazy dream state that brushes the panic aside. Because that's all this is. A dream. This feels too good to ignore, and from the safety of my own mind, I hurt no one and nothing.

The gamey taste of the bar man's fingers crawl up my throat, choking me as they make their way into my mouth. A coppery tang slides down my throat once again as I choke the appendages down a second time, forcing them back into their prison within me. They knot in my throat, as if twisting together, before dissolving and entering my stomach.

My breathing is haggard as relief comes over me that those horrific digits are gone, until the stroke of a finger down the *inside* of my stomach makes me gasp. The digit swirls around my navel. When I look down I expect the covers to be flush against my body, but they're tented over me. As if there's someone on top of me holding them up with their body. My nightgown is shoved up under my arms, and I watch a lump emerge from my stomach, just below my navel. Like something moving under a blanket, it trails across my abdomen before disappearing into my body.

The ghost hands wraps tighter around my throat, and my pussy drips with pleasure. A face flickers over me, the image coming and going with my fluttering vision. There are no defined features in the dark. Soft hair brushes against my cheek and warm hands grab my breast and tweak my nipple until pain slices through my body.

The entity inside me presses against my womb from within as the weight on top of me presses down. It slides along my inner walls, massaging my most sensitive spot. A hand spreads open then clenches shut inside me, the pressure excruciating and delicious. It slides out and in, out and in. It expands and contracts over and over again, fucking me in impossible ways while the phantom weighing me down pumps into my ass. They're using my tissue and fat and muscle against me, and I want more of it.

Iron coats my lips, the cloying thickness of blood filling my mouth as my body rocks to the pleasure it's receiving. The hand on my neck clenches harder as fingers wend their way back up my throat again as if reaching out from within me, massaging the back of my tongue. Hardly any air gets through. Black speckles my vision. My brain starts to fire as it fades, trying to get my body to buck. To fight. But I am immobile. Held in place by ghosts from outside and from within. My body hums with pleasure even as my thoughts scramble, and I gasp for air.

Phantom Nathaniel and the devil's hands fill me to bursting, and yet I want to be packed with more. There's room enough in my cells. In my organs. In my soul. I am so empty, a soulless puppet of a person left adrift when her masters died. These devilish creatures don't fill me nearly enough.

Just when I detach from my body and see myself from above, my lips blue and my eyes bulging as feeling seeps from my limbs, the orgasm explodes. Fireworks burst in front of my eyes, and my cries echo around the room as if nothing was stopping me from using my voice in the first place.

My pussy throbs with the release, my skin sizzling with the feelings of a thousand touches. My insides are liquid, pulverized by ghosts. The world fades to black as my consciousness disappears.

When my eyes open again, daylight filters through the balcony doors. I'm curled into the duvet, my nightgown intact. A frown pulls down my brows as I sit up. I gently touch my neck, but there are no signs of bruising. I cup my sex, trying to feel the after-effects of such a malicious fucking, but there's nothing. Just my body waking up for another morning. It *was* just a dream. A vivid, brutal, delicious dream.

I shuffle to the balcony doors and, with trembling hands, throw back the locks. When I open them, a well-manicured yard greets me, the haze-coated ocean and a quiet boardwalk in the distance. Morning sun struggles through the low clouds, and I know it's going to be another semi-dreary day in Shadow Cove.

I tiptoe to my door. Last night, this door was locked from the outside. I know it. I was awake for that. My hand shakes as I rest it on the handle, and I brace myself as I turn it.

It releases like any other door, opening up to the corridor and the landing.

My mind starts to second-guess itself. Maybe that was part of the dream too. But it wasn't. I know it wasn't.

It *wasn't*.

"What the fuck is going on?" I mutter to myself.

Maybe all this alone time is letting me get too deep into my mind. Perhaps I'm not processing things the right way, and this is what happens when I try to do something myself.

Or perhaps this is exactly right. This is what *I* decide, not anyone else.

I rest my hand over the apex at my thighs. A tiny pulse of pleasure throbs through me, leaving confusion in its wake. Despite my aggressive dreaming, I'm well-rested and relaxed, if not a little muddled in my mind.

Maybe this is Little Sister's way of helping me to untie the knots in my head after all.

Girl, don't make me send out a hunting party for you. I'm over here thinking you're dead. You're not dead, right? Please confirm otherwise. Shadow Cove is about to get invaded.

7

"THANK YOU FOR AGREEING TO COME WITH ME. IT'S the least I can do. I've been a terrible host. Away all the time," Mina says, her words gushing like a river as we amble along the unpaved road to town.

The unpaved, *lit* road.

"Please, it's nothing. Everything I've needed I've found. It's been great. Really," I tell her while brushing off the unsettling images that keep flickering at the edges of my vision. Not even the streetlights can push them away.

Mina doesn't need to know about my hallucinations, if that's what they are. Or whether I've just been so exhausted by my life that I'm dreaming while wide awake. I spent the day at the beach with nothing but a book and copious amounts of snacks. I had the sand to myself, and even though Shadow Cove still had a hazy film smeared over it, I enjoyed the lap of the ocean at the shore and the caw of the occasional seagull as it flew by. I tried to ignore the dearth of residents around town, the lack of cars on the road, and the missing bustle of daily life, however unsuccessfully. Shadow Cove truly seems to not come awake until nightfall.

I keep my eyes forward as we walk past the bar, my heart thundering, terror shuddering just under my skin at the thought of seeing that man again. But even from the corner of my eye I can tell he's not there. The disappointment that flashes through my chest unnerves me while the memory of him looking up at me from the yard of Little Sister's sends a twinge of desire pulsing between my legs. I swallow hard and keep pace with Mina as she chatters, pulling my mind away from the haunting specter.

The closer we get to the amusements, the more people crowd the sidewalks. Signs of life dot the storefronts. Music thumps out of a nearby restaurant, and I can even hear the screams of riders as the rollercoaster cars barrel down the hill. Smells of brine, frying fats, and sugary sweets swirl through my nose, making my mouth water.

"This is my favorite place, next to the house, of course," Mina says with a wide smile, her curls wild in the ocean breeze.

Wind flutters through her flowing skirt that just brushes her ankles. As she reaches up to tame her hair, her crop exposes a wide swath of browned skin across her stomach and the smallest peek of the swell of her breast unburdened by a bra. Pert nipples push through her thin top, but she doesn't seem to care as she glances at the lights and colors and settles serenely into the bustle of the boardwalk.

"It seems like fun," I tell her as I, too, take in the scenery.

It's an old amusement park, the wooden slats underfoot weather-beaten and splintered. The game booths are brightly colored, the lights shining like tiny suns. Only the closer I get, the cracked paint on the row of clown heads grows more obvious, their mouths gaping open and waiting for the players to shoot water at them. The rings of the ring toss are old and brown, and the strength test, and the hammer itself used to smash on the giant button anchored into the planks, looks like something from the turn of the last century, let alone this one. Still, it's a living thing we walk through. A stark contrast from the graveyard it turns into during the day.

"Come on," Mina says, her eyes bright, as she buys us both all access tickets.

I try to give her money, but she won't have it. She brushes me off and drags me to the rollercoaster. We end up in the front car, my head rushing as the panic swells, and we climb the hill. As soon as the cars descend, we open our mouths and scream, our hands clasped together as if it's the only way to keep our bodies from flying out. Our hands are still entwined as she pulls me from the car and drags me to the next ride.

The Scrambler, a ride with long seats that swirl in smaller circles as the whole ride spins, forcing riders into each other like they're in a centrifuge, is our next thrill. I sit on the inside and Mina sits at my hip. As soon as the ride starts spinning, she grabs my leg, her fingers hooking around my thigh as we yell and scream with the speed of it. I shimmy my arm from under me and wrap it around her, hugging her tighter as her hand inches up my leg. My yelps at the ride hide the smile trying to bloom on my face at her touch.

Gone are the haunting images of the man from the bar, the murder of the old caretakers of Little Sister's, and the penetrating stare of Owen, Mina's electrician. There is just Mina and her hands on me and the thrill of the carnival wrapping us in its neon embrace.

She insists on cotton candy before we take our seats on the Ferris wheel. There is plenty of space in the carriage, but we sit touching, thigh to thigh. Mina rips a bit of cotton candy off the paper spear and holds it out to my mouth, a smile on her face. We lurch to a start, the car moving backward before it swings us up and around. Without thinking, I open my mouth, the invitation she needs to place the sticky floss on my tongue. Her finger brushes my lip as she deposits it, and my tongue touches the tips of her fingers as she leaves me to the sweetness. I laugh as it dissolves on my tongue, the sugary hit briefly reminding me of the man's fingers as they dissolved into my body. I brush the image away and lean into Mina, where she feeds me more sticky treats.

Our ride ends too soon, and so does the cotton candy. As we wander the boardwalk—shoulder to shoulder, always touching—she points to something I don't catch, grabs my hand, and takes off at a run. I stumble at first but catch myself after a couple steps and easily keep pace with her until we reach an old-fashioned funhouse. The mechanical cackling laughter of an ancient talking head bellows over us. An exaggerated smile leers at us, its eyes round and searching as its jaw unhinges as it laughs.

"We have to go in there. It's so much fun. I swear it's my favorite amusement," Mina says with a wide smile showing gleaming white teeth.

"This is?" I ask skeptically, as I gaze around at the funhouse monolith.

It's a two-story building shuttered to anyone on the outside wanting to look in. Garish colors and swirling fonts adorn its facade. The entrance is a giant clown's mouth, jagged teeth up top as if it'll bite everyone walking in and swallow them whole. As I'm weighing my options, the door at the far end slams open, and a group of teenage girls tumbles out, laughing and screeching.

"See?" Mina says, pointing to the group. "It'll be fun. I promise."

A feeling settles into my stomach like a stone, something I

can't quite name. Apprehension. Reluctance. Nervousness. At what, I don't know. Maybe I'm afraid the whole thing will collapse with us in it. It looks old enough to be held together with little more than duct tape and a dream. But as Mina grabs my hand and motions to the entrance, I find I can't deny her. A smile flickers at my lips. The warmth of her hand radiates up my arm as she guides me to the ticket taker. We show the bored attendant our wristbands and enter the funhouse.

Calliope music filters through unseen speakers, tinny, wheezing jangles that meld together to form some semblance of a song struggling to reach its end. Still, it reminds me of when Quinn and I would go to the local fair. We'd been going every year since high school. I smile at the thought, then remember I haven't heard from her since I got here. Between the shitty cell service and the spotty Wi-Fi wherever I go, I don't know if any of my messages have gotten out.

Before I can think more about it, Mina yanks my hand and pulls me into the dark. The deeper we go into the funhouse shadows, the less amusing it all is and the more ominous it grows. Dots of neon pink lights and an ever-shrinking box of an entry wraps us in its clutches.

There's no way back but onward now.

Mina steps forward and stumbles but laughs a full-throated laugh as she braces herself against the moving walls and shuffles forward. My eyes adjust enough to see I'm walking through a spinning barrel. I stumble too as I step into it. A chuckle escapes my lips as I find my footing and follow Mina inside.

A cackling, animatronic clown lunges at us, its gears just as loud as its guffaws. We both screech before falling into each other's arms laughing. My heart hammers, making my head woozy, fright and adrenaline spinning in each beat as we hold each other and continue on.

Black swirling lights and squishy floors eventually lead up a set of stairs into a labyrinth of mirrors. Our faces multiply into infinity as they stare back at us, around us, behind us.

"Oooooo my favorite! Stay close or you'll get lost!" Mina says with a bounce in her step as she enters the maze.

I try to stay on her heels, but my eyes are pulled in a million directions as dozens of Lucys and Minas flash in and out of sight. The further we go into the maze, the more warped the mirrors get, our bodies twisting and distorting in the reflections. Mina's laugh echoes around me. I laugh back and reach out to her only to bump against a mirror.

She disappears from the reflection and appears in another. I reach out again and meet cold metal, only my face looking back at me.

"Mina?" I call out. All I hear in return is the haunting calliope music and the fading echo of Mina's laugh.

"Mina?" I try again, but it's only my voice now.

Every step I take I hit a dead end. Reflecting glass closes in on me, edges leading to more dead ends. The exhilaration melts from my face, replaced with wide eyes growing wider and my mouth turning down. The lights meant to lead me out of the labyrinth spin me in circles. I'm more turned around than ever.

Until I see *him*.

A dark silhouette in the mirror. A figure clad all in black. He steps forward, under the shine of a purple light, and it casts a glow across his angular face. His stare is only for me as he moves forward. My heartbeat picks up, panic choking me as I feel my way along the glass, scrambling to make my way through the maze of mirrors.

When I look behind me he's gone. I stop and look around, not believing what I'm seeing. Or not seeing. Until a flicker catches in the corner of my eye, and he appears in another mirror. Just one. He isn't reflected into infinity like I am. It's as if he exists from within the looking glass, not out.

I back into a wall of reflection, the glass cold through my shirt. I can hardly breathe as the man disappears again only to reappear in another mirror, as if he moves through panes of glass.

A hand moves along my side and wraps around my stomach. I gasp at the touch. A shush hisses at my ear as fingers slither along my neck and wrap tight around my throat, holding me to the cold glass.

"Don't worry, Lucy. Let us take care of you," the whisper says, breath hot on my ear.

I turn my head just enough to see the outline of a nose and the full lips of Mina's electrician. The glass waves as he presses through it, the warmth of his body replacing the cold mirror. His heat lasts only a moment before the chill presses into my back as he pulls me closer to him, the two of us straddling two worlds.

Owen.

"Don't hurt me," I mutter, as his hands hold me tighter, the touch of him shooting fear and desire through my veins.

"Never," he whispers back, as he runs his nose along my neck, his tongue tasting my flesh.

I turn into him. Owen wraps his body around me, bringing himself more into my world and me more into his. Half of my back, my shoulder, and the upper half of my arm to my elbow are submerged in a shuddering chill before I realize I can't move. Owen pulls me even closer, sinking my ear, my cheek, and one eye into the mirror world he emerged from, as if we're changing places. The calliope music dims and the flashing carnival lights dull as my senses mute in this other world, the rest of me stuck with Owen's roaming hands. I try tugging free of the glass, but it holds me firm. Like I'm frozen in ice, but Owen's electric kisses jolt heat through me. The press of his lips at my neck and the graze of his hands along my body pushing the chill mirror world away.

Aiden appears in the mirror in front of me, then steps through it as if he's pushing through a film. The dissonance of calliope music grows louder. Red emergency lights slash sinister shadows across his face as he reaches for me and plants his lips against mine. The voice in my mind must be trapped in the mirror, because it's muffled. I know it tries to tell me to fight, but Aiden's lips play against mine, and I can't help but respond. My free hand grasps the lapel of his jacket to pull him closer, encouraging him to join Owen in mapping my body with his lips. Me being trapped in a mirror doesn't appear to register for him.

Or for me for that matter.

Pressure releases as the button on my pants pops. The zipper shudders against my abdomen as Aiden drags it down. Panic flutters through my mind at being discovered. Followed closely by a drenching thrill of being seen, held hostage by glass and being ravaged by men who emerged from its ether.

Only I know no one will be stumbling upon us. I know it like I know the questionable reality of the phantom fucking I received last night. There is nothing here, not to anyone else. Somehow these men—like the phantom, like that man from the bar—have distorted time. We don't exist in this funhouse. We exist beyond it so long as these men desire it. They've pulled me into their world. A world where reality is immaterial, my sanity is inconsequential, and they play with me much like predators play with their prey. They get off on it as much as I get off on them doing it.

My bare ass hits cold glass as my pants, along with my underwear, disappear. Fingers find openings and probe and push, forcing mewling moans from my throat just as a hand gently wraps around it. A thumb lands on my clit and swirls, but I don't know who it belongs to.

I don't care.

A gentle pressure presses at my back before my insides swirl with delight, strummed by previously-consumed fingers probing my atoms. It's a pressure just this side of pain, but I'm stroked inside and out in ways I didn't think possible. There's another gentle pressure from within my stomach. I glance down as far as I can see in my captive state, and witness the press of fingers along my flesh, vying to come out. Much like the movement I saw last night with the phantom.

Each press is like a lick to my most sensitive spots, and I let out a moan as the fingers push and stroke. With one final push, pressure releases and I gasp with the exquisiteness of it. It's the cresting wave of an orgasm denied, and it leaves me gasping. I glance down again to find a hand protruding from my middle, coated with thick blood and bits of flesh.

I choke. Panic floods my veins as a keening wail builds in my throat. Until Owen's gentle breath on my skin dissolves my terror.

"You are delicious," he whispers, as he pushes his arm through my body, blood coated to his elbow.

He holds me to him as he bends his arm and cups my sex with his blood-coated hand. One finger slides through my folds, then another, before they enter me. I lean into him, leveraging as much as I can to get him as deep as possible.

My muscles clench around his fingers—around his arm, as if the hole he broke through me is an extension of my cunt— as the delicious rhythm builds. Owen and Aiden work in tandem to kiss and lick and finger fuck me out of this reality, and I melt into them.

I fear nothing.

I'm afraid of nothing.

There is nothing for me to worry about.

Until *he* appears again, striding across mirrors as if they're doorways. Their liquidity ripples out of his way as if it's painful to be in his presence, let alone be touched by him.

A smirk pulls across his face, and my lone eye watches him approach. Owen slides another bloody finger into my cunt as Aiden finds my waiting ass and probes with one digit, then two.

Aiden's lips trail down my neck as he buries his fingers in me. His teeth nip at my tender skin before a hard bite punctures my flesh. A shout of pain bursts through my growing orgasm before entwining it. He sucks at my skin, gulps my blood in mouthfuls, before pulling away. He doesn't stay away long, and his teeth sink into my flesh once again, expanding the wound he just made. His tongue slides through the torn flesh, and it feels like a tongue stroking my pussy. Shudders ripple across my body as he licks the fading pain away.

The man from the bar holds my gaze as his hand trails down my stomach to where Owen's arm rests within my torso. He slides his fingers into my body, grazing Owen's arm, and I shudder at the touch. It's as divine as Owen. As blissful as Aiden. The man probes my body torn asunder and waves of pleasure wash through me. The feeling of him entering me is so familiar yet foreign. Enticing and unwelcome. He enters where he pleases, and I take it all the same.

He slides his fingers in and out of the wound before he disappears from sight. When a mouth—hot and moist—latches onto my cunt, I know it's him as he devours me. Owen's arm turns within me, flesh and sinew squelching with the movement. I shudder at the sounds, growing wetter with each muscle twitch. Owen's hand slides up my body, moving my shirt out of the way and exposing a breast. Fingers slick with my juices and dripping in my blood grab it. Massage it.

He takes a nipple between two bloody fingers and twists. My knees would buckle if I didn't already have Aiden and the man from the bar holding me up and the mirror suspending me between two worlds.

A yell chokes me, and the orgasm continues to build. The rollercoaster car forever climbing the hill, never quite reaching the top. The man's tongue probes and licks as his teeth nip sensitive flesh. Nips turn to bites, all teeth and tongues and sucking and licking. It's a never-ending dance of feasting as the men consume me to my marrow.

All the while the orgasm builds.

Owen bites onto the other side of my neck, the pinch of his jaw powerful, while Aiden moves to a breast. He takes the bloody nipple in his mouth and his teeth sink into my fatty flesh. The snap and pop of skin makes me buck, desperate to drive them all in deeper. I teeter on the brink of reality, my body torn open and eaten, and me desperate to offer more of my flesh to them. It's a vivid dream I can't possibly be having.

Owen's arm moves inside of me while he sucks at my shoulder, pushing aside liver and kidneys and stomach to hold my breast for Aiden. Moans flitter past my lips as they consume me. They could cut me into pieces and serve me on a platter, and I would beg for it. The slide of fingers in and out of my pussy is the same luscious feeling as Owen sliding his arm through my stomach. Aiden's probing of my ass is just as delicious as the nameless man burying his face in my cunt and eating me down to the womb.

I ate him. Now he consumes me, face buried and teeth tearing through labia. But the pieces of him inside me, swimming through my veins, know what buttons of mine to push. The slow bloom of pain is immediately replaced by the cresting pleasure of a tongue-flicked clit. The cold wave of blood loss is replaced by a flash of heat so intense I swoon, falling further into Owen's arms as he holds me up. My head swims with it all.

The lights flash, blinding bright white. My eyes flutter with the sudden light before darkness settles back over me. Through bobbing heads and gnashing jaws, a woman moves out of the shadows. She's petite with a mass of curly hair on top of her head. Only now, instead of a flowing skirt and crop top, she's naked as she moves through the mirrors like the men did. She follows no path except the one through impossible glass toward me. The calliope music slows to a broken dirge as she approaches.

Blood slashes across her breasts and stomach. Her pubic hair drips with it, and it trails down her legs. It coats her chin and dribbles down her neck. She raises one hand to her mouth and sticks three fingers in. Her lips wrap around the digits as she holds my gaze, the look sending a pulse through my core.

Mina.

The missing piece to our carnival feast.

My orgasm keeps building, the crest only growing ever higher as the men eat, and Mina closes in.

Deep brown eyes hold my one good eye as she closes the distance. My fingers twitch and my lashes flutter, but that is all the movement I can make. What pieces of me aren't trapped in the mirror are clamped in the mouths of monsters. A moan escapes my throat as she stands in front of me, her proximity making me desperate.

Licking cotton candy from her fingers. Our touching thighs. My arm around her shoulders. Her hand moving up my leg. I want her in the most desperate of ways.

The man at my feet wraps a hand around her leg when she gets close enough. The movement doesn't deter him from his meal as he pulls a strip of flesh from my cunt and swallows it whole. His fingers inch toward her pussy before submerging into her core, plugging her into us, this bloody organism. Mina runs her hand through his hair as she opens her stance to give him better access.

She runs a finger down the center of my chest and swirls it around the one free nipple. I choke on my breaths, the pleasure overwhelming. I don't know how much more I can take, but my body expands, opens even more as faces and mouths and limbs bury themselves within me. I want nothing but more of it. More of them. More of her. I've never felt freer than in this moment of wanting and taking.

We stand eye to eye as she drags a finger up my neck and places two fingers on my bottom lip. My mouth opens, and she slides them across my tongue, massaging the thickness of it as I wrap my lips around her and moan. She pulls herself free of my mouth and drags a finger back down my throat. There's a gentle pressure on my neck before a hot slice of pain lances down my spine. It lasts only a moment before the devilry inside me sets to work, turning the hurt to desperate need. My senses flare with pleasure, and whatever worry I might have had resolves into the blood pooling around my feet.

Mina's mouth hangs open in a pleasurable O as she slides her finger into the slice she just made in my throat. In and out, the slow and steady rhythm builds the desire in my pussy, much the same way Owen's arm through my middle feels like a gratifying fuck. In a moment of clarity, my brain scrambles through the feelings, tries comprehending what's happening to me. She cut me, sliced through my body, yet it feels divine. She watches herself, her finger sliding in and out of the hole she created, before she bites her lip, looks at me, and slides another finger in.

She turns her hands up and curls her fingers as she probes the hole, and my pussy pulses as if she's stroking me so much lower. I groan, my body writhing with the motion as much as it can. The tips of her fingers hit the back of my throat, and I choke. It's not air I desire. It's *her*. She slides a third finger in and my pussy fills with the feeling of *her*. Of *them*. The man's mouth eats his way across my cunt. Aiden has consumed one breast down to the muscle. His tongue sliding through the meat feels like it's probing my G-spot directly. Owen pulls my flesh from my collarbone and runs his tongue along the bone. He probes at the vertebrae at the base of my neck, flicking his tongue between the discs, and I pant with desire, desperate for release.

The pleasure builds, an ever-growing mountain, and I wonder if I'll ever come down from it.

"Soon," Mina whispers, as she slides her fingers in and out of my throat, the squelch of blood and flesh sending my desire dripping down my leg. Or perhaps that's more blood. "You will be so much more than what you are."

She leans forward. I anticipate the press of her lips against mine. Instead, she flicks out her tongue and probes the hole in my neck with her fingers still inside. She licks at the rim of the wound and uses her fingers to spread it wide. She shoves her tongue into the gap, deeper into me, and my body quivers.

My pussy pulses with desire, the throb of it nearly unbearable. If I didn't know any better in my brain-addled state, I'd think Mina was controlling my orgasm. My climax is in Mina's hands, and I will only get it if I give in to her.

I want her to have it—all of it—so, so badly.

The bastard feeling of reality flashes through my mind. My real-world obligations. The expectations set upon me by everyone but me. The dutiful daughter. The overachieving employee. The best friend. My life has never been my own. For the first time, I am faced with a decision that only I must make. No one else matters. It's with that revelation that I float. If I weren't being held in place by monsters of the night picking the flesh from my bones, I would soar away.

I want to unravel. I want to dissolve. To be unmade and piece myself back together again in something that feels better than what I've been. Something that speaks to me. That makes sense. Everything here—now—makes sense.

"Do you want us, Lucy? Do you want to be *more*?" Mina whispers, but her voice is a boom in my ear.

My breath shudders, and I finally find my own voice. "More," I mutter. My one eye watches the vicious smile that curls across Mina's face. "More." It's the only word I can form.

She pulls her hand away from me and slides the bloody fingers into her mouth. Full lips wrap around the digits, and she slides her fingers in and out as she cleans me from her flesh. From one beat to the next, Mina snarls and plunges her fist into the hole in my throat. The orgasm crashes over me in a tidal wave. It's an explosion of light, then complete darkness as I finally crest and fall over the edge. There's nothing but hands and mouths and probing and fucking, and I gasp and moan with the pleasure of it all.

The lights flicker, and the funhouse comes back to life. The calliope music whirls back to a normal speed. I gasp and fall against the nearest wall of mirrors. They're as clear as day, reflecting nothing but me back at myself. Tinny clown laughter echoes over the glass maze. The dead end I'm huddled in is empty, cold, and lifeless. It's only my frazzled face that looks out at me from the looking glass. My breath fogs the surface as I pant, trying not to hyperventilate.

My hands scrabble across my midsection, but my stomach is intact. I claw at my throat, but there's no hole. My clothes are still on, my face is not stuck in a mirror world, but my pussy throbs with spent desire. I press my hand to my apex and feel the pulse of my cunt as the orgasm subsides. With each struggling breath I get in a little more air and my head starts to clear.

Teenage cackles ring through the space, lurching me even further from the delirium I'm crawling out of. I lean my head against the nearest mirror and revel in the chill that seeps through my skin, only to wrench it back as I remember how I sunk into the glass and it held me there while I . . . whatever happened, happened.

I reach out a shaking hand and press a finger to another mirror pane only to be met with solid reality. I look at myself pointing at myself through the mirror. Replicas of me multiplied into infinity. It really is just me and the mirrors in the fucking funhouse.

"Lucy, there you are!" Mina says as she rounds a mirrored corner, concern writ across her face. "I thought you got swallowed whole. That was a spooky thirty seconds, wasn't it?"

Mina walks closer and I frown, trying to comprehend what she just said and failing. "Thirty seconds?"

A frown mars her beautiful face, but she tries to smile through it. "Yes, when the power went out. It wasn't long, but in here it felt like forever." A light chuckle escapes her, and her frown deepens. "Are you okay? I think you're sweating."

She reaches out. The flash of her wicked smile. Blood dripping from her fingers as she licks them clean. But she's only reaching, waiting for my reaction. I remain still. Frozen. Until she gently brushes her thumb along my forehead and pulls away a bead of sweat. A piece of me expects her to bring her thumb to her mouth and taste the salty moisture of me. Instead, she drops her hand to her side and waits for my response.

"Yeah—" I clear my throat. "Yes. Sorry. Just had a moment. Some sea air and I'll be fine."

It's a lie, thick and cloying on my tongue, but she wouldn't believe me if I told her the truth. That I think I'm breaking, and she is the hammer shattering me.

Mina nods and threads her fingers through mine before guiding me out of the mirror maze, through a neon hellscape, across a hamster wheel, and out onto the boardwalk once more.

The world keeps going out here. Children rush past. Couples stroll along the gangway. Rich smells of chocolate and fried dough fill the air. It all helps to push the images from my mind, as does Mina's warm hand in mine. She's the one anchoring me to this earth. The only one. I feel like I'm about to float away, and Mina is the one holding the string.

She doesn't press. Doesn't ask questions. She lets me be. Lets me sit with myself as she gets us drinks, and I wonder what the hell happened in that funhouse. What the hell is happening to me? My core throbs, and I press my hand to my abdomen, ripping flesh and gnashing teeth wending their way through thrill-seeker screams and ringing bells from the carnival games. I can almost convince myself it's all in my head.

Almost.

I'M CALLING THE POLICE

To: QuinnMorrisEsq@helsinglaw.com
From: LucyWest87@nightshademail.com

I don't know how to get a hold of you. You're not answering my emails. Only half my texts get delivered. The rest die in my phone for whatever fucking reason. And Google says Little Sister's doesn't exist. When I pull the address up on Maps it's nothing but a vacant lot with an old foundation.

WHERE THE FUCK ARE YOU?

I'm really starting to get worried, and that subject line is a lie. I already called the police. They didn't take me seriously. They said to stop bothering you on your retreat and brushed me off. Fucking assholes.

I'll fly out there if I have to. You can't have just disappeared. Please, Luce. Answer me. Please. You're scaring me. I have the worst feeling that something's wrong.

Please don't let something be wrong.

Go to the library or something, get on some decent Wi-Fi, and email me back. Something. Please.

Q

8

"I INSIST. GO UP TO YOUR ROOM, GET INTO something comfy, and I'll bring you some tea. Whatever scare you had in the funhouse, you don't seem to have gotten over it. Go! I'm not taking no for an answer," Mina says, pointing up the stairs with a laugh on her lips.

Brushing off my incident in the funhouse has been impossible. The images, the feelings, the finish, all haunt my mind and refuse to be shaken. Phantom hands slither along my skin and inside my body. Warm lips and wet tongues caress me when there's nothing there.

I just need to lie down. Whatever is happening in my head needs to be sorted, likely by a professional, but that will need to wait until I get home.

If I go home.

I stop halfway up the stairs. The thought is jarring. I don't know where it comes from. *Of course I'm going home*, I chastise myself. *Why wouldn't I?*

The pictures on the wall draw my eye, especially Nathaniel's. My skin pebbles with the memories of his ghost on top of me, caressing me. Bringing me to heights I've never reached before. Heat rushes my cheeks. Just as my focus falters, the edges of the frames going fuzzy, the photograph of Nathaniel winks.

I jerk away from the wall and stumble into the railing, my foot slipping off the stair before I can pull myself together. The manic beating of my heart steals the breath from my lungs. I press my hand to my chest to try and slow the engine down while I stare at the picture.

Waiting.

"Everything okay?" Mina asks, her head popping around the wall that hides the kitchen.

"Yeah. I'm okay. I think I'm just tired," I mutter and try to smile. I can't possibly look more frazzled than I have since coming out of the funhouse.

If my episode at the boardwalk isn't something to hide, imagining a picture coming to life certainly is.

Mina smiles back, her look pained. "I'll be up in a minute with your tea. Go relax."

I nod and carry on up the stairs, my feet heavy and my head full. I pull out my silk robe, grateful for this small piece of luxury I brought with me. The fabric glides through my fingers and is a cool relief as I settle it against my bare body. Even light footsteps make the stairs creak as Mina walks to my room and gently knocks on my door.

"It's unlocked," I say. The door clicks as she opens it.

She leaves it open, and I don't ask her to close it. There's no one else here. In theory, at least. There is *something* else here, in this house. Some kind of presence lingering in my periphery. I just can't get a good look at it.

Mina sets the tea tray on a side table, steam rising from the teacup. She pads closer and sits next to me, the mattress dipping with her weight. Her body is a comfort despite what I saw her do in my mind. A violent image of a violent mind's creation, only I never knew my head was capable of thinking such things.

I shake it away. That's not Mina. Mina is a proprietor of an inn in a small beach town, not some . . . whatever the fuck she was in the fever dream my head created.

"Give it a few minutes. It's boiling hot. I wouldn't want you to burn your mouth," she says, her voice soft.

Her eyes dip to my lips before they find my gaze again, and she smiles.

"Are you sure you don't want to talk about it?" she asks after a motionless moment of silence.

I do want to talk about it, but I'm afraid what she'll think of me. I don't need to burden her with the mess in my head. But the room warms the longer she sits next to me. The press of her thigh against mine. The heat of her dissolving my tension and my barriers.

My gaze finds hers, and we stare at each other for an interminably long moment. Time seems to stand still in the space between us. Until I stand, my body anxious despite my brain's calm, and walk to the balcony. The handle on the double door is cool to the touch as I pull it open.

"I don't want to unload all my nonsense onto you. At least not before I figure it out myself," I say with a laugh.

"Sometimes confiding in others can help you feel less lost and alone," she says to my back.

I pull the door the rest of the way open and freeze.

The man stands in the backyard, cloaked in shadow yet his body is unmistakable. The outline of it. The glint of pale hair in the moonlight struggling through the growing fog. The flare of his cigarette as he pulls from it.

"Who is that?" I whisper more to myself than to Mina, but

she's at my shoulder in a heartbeat. A comforting presence wrapping around me. Protecting me from *him*.

I expect her to look over my shoulder and see nothing but darkness. As her face comes into my periphery and she smiles, I know she sees him too. And she knows him.

"Caleb," she whispers, as she pulls back, her face no longer visible as I keep my gaze pointed out the door.

"He keeps haunting me," I whisper back. "They all do." I turn my head to look at Mina, curiosity writ across her features with a sly smile hanging on the corner of her mouth. "You too."

"Are you afraid?" she asks. Her eyes graze my lips as the hem of my robe slides up my legs.

"Yes." I shudder as I look back out the balcony door.

Caleb stands there. I can't see his face, but I know he's looking at me. At us. Wind flutters at my core as I realize the robe has been pulled all the way up. Mina's hand grazes my ass, and I have to suppress a shiver.

"This isn't fear I'm seeing," she whispers, as her nose glances up the side of my neck. Her hand ventures lower, over the curve of my ass and between my legs.

"This isn't fear I feel." She slides her hands along my slit, slicking herself with my arousal as my heart thunders in my chest.

"What is this place?" I choke out. One finger finds its way inside me, and Mina gasps as I gasp. "What's happening to me?"

Another finger slips into me, and I step my legs apart to give her better access. She runs her free hand along the opening of my robe and pulls the hem to the side, exposing a breast to Caleb and the night I'm supposed to fear and respect.

"My home is everything you need and everything you want," Mina says, her voice breathy against my ear.

Tingles scatter along my neck, and the little hairs rise at her words. Her fingers probe me, sliding in and out of my core as if they were my own. She knows what I like, how I like it, and my knees buckle with the pleasure. I lean forward and grasp the wrought iron railing, spreading my legs wider. Begging with my body.

Mina steps closer, takes my exposed breast in her free hand, and twists the hardened nipple. A moan escapes my throat as I arch my back and press into her driving hand. She twists the nipple harder and tugs at the sensitive flesh as she looks at the shadowy Caleb figure still in the yard, still watching us. My body moves with her hand. I grind into her fingers just as she slips a third one in, and I gasp with the pressure of it.

"You wouldn't have found us if you weren't looking." Mina fucks me harder, her fingers grinding into me and me helpless against her touch.

Reason escapes me. Logic has left the building. I want nothing more than to be fucked by Mina as Caleb watches. As a piece of him swims inside of me and lights me up from the inside.

"You have nothing to fear from us." She probes me harder and faster, my orgasm building with each thrust. "Do you fear us?"

Who is us? The question fades from my mind, replaced by the wandering hands of Mina and her men as pleasure overwhelms me. Mina fucks away my concerns and my reservations and my fears. Caleb and Aiden and Owen scare the shit out of me. But I want nothing more than to feel this invincible forever.

"No," I mutter.

Mina's fingers disappear from within, the bloom of my orgasm fading with every passing second, and I groan.

She holds her glistening fingers in front of her before putting them in her mouth and sucking them clean. "Good."

Her hand lashes out and grasps my jaw in a harsh grip before pulling me to her. Our lips smash together, and I'm lost in her kiss. It's a ferocious, needy thing as our tongues tangle. Teeth scrape against flesh, and the subtle taste of copper trickles into my mouth. I grab Mina's head and hold her to me as I explore her mouth and press my body to hers.

My robe slides from my shoulders, leaving me standing naked in front of her, in front of the night, and just within sight of Caleb who surely still watches us. I pull her shirt over her head, and she gladly lifts her arms to help. There is no bra to remove, and her pert breasts bounce with the release. I can't help but run my fingers along her light brown flesh. Her breath quickens with the touch. I graze my fingers along her bare back. Slide my hand down the back of her pants to cup her ass and press her closer to me.

Her loose-fitting pants slide off easily, leaving the two of us wrapped in nothing but each other. I back Mina to the bed. She willingly goes, bouncing on the mattress as I crawl over her and lay atop her gorgeous body. We lie entwined for a moment, the heat between us growing, before my lips wander down her neck, her collarbone, her chest. I slide down to take one breast in my mouth as I play with the other. Mina arches into me, and I take a nipple between my teeth, reveling in her moans.

A hand brushes my cheek, the touch tender and inviting, before fingers tangle in my hair and fist. A gentle pressure on my head tells me to go lower. I gladly obey as I slide down her body, planting kisses as I go.

The black tuft of hair between her legs is neatly trimmed, and her sex is swollen and inviting, a lush pink waiting to be probed. I run my tongue along her slit. Mina gasps and spreads her legs wider. My tongue maneuvers between her folds, licking and flicking each piece of her, learning her as she responds to my caresses.

My finger plays at her wet entrance before I slide it in, the heat of her pulsing desire in my core. It's quickly followed by a second as I curl my fingers inside her and press my mouth to her clit and suck. Moans and low-throated growls roll out of her as she holds my head in place. I slide in and out of her, licking all of her sensitive places as I move with her body.

Until something catches my eye as I tilt my head. Something bright red and coating my fingers. Through Mina's panting I pull my hand away and find my fingers covered in blood, red and fresh. I taste nothing but her arousal, but the sight of the blood stirs something within me. Caleb's consumed fingers respond, stroking sensitive places from inside my body, beckoning the outside in.

"Mina," I whisper, as I hold up my hand.

She glances at it, and then my face, my hair still firmly controlled in her grip. "Oh," she whispers, her eyes large and glinting.

I can't tell what the look is, but the *urge* comes over me. A nudge like someone pressing my elbow up to get my fingers closer to my mouth. A look settles across Mina's face—desire and will—an unspoken demand. I bring my bloodied fingers to my mouth and wrap my lips around them.

Fireworks explode behind my eyes. The subtle taste of pussy and copper fills my mouth along with something altogether otherworldly. My skin buzzes with life, sings with it. I feel like I could float away if Mina weren't holding me down.

I lick my fingers clean and look up at my captor, a sly smile curling across her face. The high fades too quickly, and just as it's tapering off, Mina's gentle pressure on my head returns. I lower my face to her cunt, the smell of blood igniting a fire in me, and I dive into her.

My tongue probes her entrance, my need to consume her unparalleled. I run my tongue up and down her folds, her blood a divine elixir as I devour this beautiful woman laid out before me. I can't get enough of her, this delicious drug taking over my veins. Cackles and moans bleed together in a symphony of pleasure as Mina grows more vocal, her hold on me tightening.

After a handful of minutes she goes rigid, her moans turning to choking gasps as she comes. I continue to lap at her, taking everything she can give me. Swallowing it down as if it's life itself. The pressure on my head releases. I'm winded as Mina crawls onto my lap, my fingers back in my mouth as I lick every drop of blood from my flesh.

She leans down, her lips just brushing mine until she presses a finger to my mouth. "My turn," she says with a smile as she pushes me back onto the bed, and I gladly give in to her.

Mina's blood courses through my veins as her lips trail down my chest. She takes one breast in her mouth. At first she gently suckles, then flicks at the hardened nipple. Teeth find the tender flesh and clamp, lightly as first, then harder and harder until I yell out, the mixture of pleasure and pain pulsing through me, dampening my thighs with my arousal.

Lips trail down my stomach before Mina's head disappears between my legs. Gentle breaths blow against my opening, a cruel tease as she flutters kisses on my thighs, on my lips, on the crease of my legs. I spread wide for her, inviting her in, quietly begging her. She obliges with a thrust of her tongue into my folds, my entrance. It's a barrage against my clit, the intensity extreme, the pleasure edging the line of pain, but I want more.

Fingers probe my opening, one then two then three, filling me as she devours me. When she pulls out, she leaves an emptiness behind that has me moaning, whimpering.

Pleading.

I rest my hand on her head. "Please, Mina." I gasp. "Please."

I *grovel*. She obliges as the sorcery of her tongue takes me to new heights, her fingers swirling inside me in waves as Caleb's digits probe from within, mixing with Mina's blood to create divinity. Blooming godlike. The funhouse was dinner. Mina is my dessert.

A sharp, piercing pain lances up my leg before warmth trickles across my skin. Mina's tongue drags along my flesh, and the pain disappears, until that sharpness returns on the other side. Thighs, lips, every inch of flesh at my apex feels the sharp pain Mina gives before she wipes it away with an ever-mounting orgasm.

Like the funhouse, I don't feel in control of my body. Mina holds me at a knife's edge, letting me teeter until she deems me worthy of finishing. And I let her. I lie back and spread my legs wider. When she looks at me—blood covering her face, and smiles—I think nothing of it other than now she matches me.

She pulls herself up, settling herself on top of me, my orgasm lingering on the precipice, and grabs both of my breasts in her bloody hands, smearing blood across my skin. I wrap my legs around her body, my flesh growing cold, and she grinds into me as she runs her tongue along the edge of my sensitive breast.

"Do you want this, Lucy?" Mina mutters around a mouthful of my blood, a piece of flesh stuck to her sharpened teeth.

I see it all, but I don't. I only observe Mina, luscious divine.

There is nothing else I want. Nothing else I need except her. I nod my acquiescence, but her black eyes glint, and her bloody hand snaps out to grab my face.

"Say it. I need to hear it from your mouth," she whispers onto my lips. I am so much putty in her hands.

"I want you, Mina," I breathe. "I'm yours."

A blood-coated smile spreads across her face as she laughs and returns her attention to my breast. She licks along the flesh, flicks at the nipple, and bites into the meat of it like biting into a ripe apple. A sharp stab cuts through my chest, and I cry out, the pain exquisite as Mina's teeth sink into me. Until she anchors her knee between my legs and grinds against me. Bone snaps as she bites and tears into my chest with a yank of her head. Her tongue slithers between ribs as Mina fucks me into oblivion. Ripping flesh blends with my moans as I grind into her knee, my orgasm peaking.

Growing higher. And higher. And higher.

One more bite—teeth like knives piercing straight through my heart—Mina's face buried in my chest, and I explode. My blood is an inferno as the room goes dark.

I gasp and sit up, the room spinning as I put my hand to my chest. There is no Mina on top of me. My robe is still tied tightly around my body. On the bedside table is a small tea service, the only indication Mina was here at all. I throw back the duvet and the sheets are clean. No bloody remnants on my fingers. No copper in my mouth. I press my hand back to my chest and pull the robe aside only to find my flesh intact.

Even the balcony door is closed, the sheer curtains hanging lifeless in front of them. What isn't lifeless is my pussy as it throbs with the aftereffects of another orgasm. Raucous and intense, I feel it in my stomach. I press my hand between my legs and feel the pulse of my muscle. Then I pat the side of my face, making sure I'm real.

That all of this is real.

The light on the other side of the window is late afternoon. The clock at my bedside tells me it's going on early evening. I slept all day and had a fuck of a dream while I was at it.

A dream that felt so incredibly real. Like the funhouse where I was devoured whole. Only now it's Mina—not a tease, but an instigator—and my falling helplessly at her feet for it.

Something is very, very wrong here.

9

My stomach rumbles as I make my way down the stairs. I catch a glimpse of my reflection in a passing mirror and brace myself for what I might see. I came to Little Sister's to rest, but I've done the opposite, and I expect it to show. Except what looks back at me is like nothing I would expect. Not after that . . . dream?

I expect my hair to be knotted and blood to coat my face. Bruises to cover my neck. But my skin is clear. Porcelain. More unblemished than when I arrived. My eyes shine with a light coming from within, my pupils dilated to big black orbs. A frenetic buzz of a look that could be excited or high. My hair is shiny, the red never having looked redder, and fuller. A complete turn-around from when I first arrived. My stomach rumbles again, and I pull myself away from the glass and carry on to the kitchen.

There's a loaf of bread on the counter. I tear into it, stuffing a piece in my mouth, expecting to savor its yeasty sweetness. Instead, it's bland, flavorless, and vaguely stale. I snatch a parfait from the fridge and much the same. I can barely taste the sweet berries, and the cultured yogurt lands flat on my tongue, gelatinous and thick.

Still, my stomach rumbles, my hunger growing by the second.

My dream haunts me. Mina's blood on my fingers, flowing into my mouth. How she feasted on my body. Fed from me. The more I think about it—the more I focus on that divine red—the more my mouth waters. My teeth ache and a pain wrenches through my gut, buckling my knees and dropping me to the floor. I groan and wince my way through the ache.

Nausea overwhelms me, and I try to breathe through it. But the more breaths I take, the stuffier the kitchen gets. My mouth waters, eager for sustenance, but nothing seems to sate my hunger.

Perhaps what I need is some fresh air. Clear my head. Let the cool ocean air chill my heated face. My heated thoughts.

An early evening sky greets me as I swing the front door open. Fog hangs low against the purple sky, obscuring the property around the house and the dangerous cliff line in the near distance. My robe flutters around my legs and arms in the refreshing breeze, the scent of brine and baked sand wafting to my nose.

I'm halfway across the yard before I realize I've taken a step, the house aglow behind me, windows like eyes against the ever-darkening sky. A bank of angry clouds rolls in, a rumble of thunder announcing the storm's arrival. A bolt of lightning streaks across the sky, and I gasp at the rot of Little Sister's that stares back at me. Instead of the pristine doll house, it's a rotted carcass of what once was. The turret has collapsed. Shaker siding is chipped or missing altogether. Dark, broken windows dot the facade. When the lightning disappears, the house goes black.

The nearby bushes rustle, and a low growl rumbles across

the grass. Footsteps rush me from the shadows, thumping against the ground as they get closer. There's only time enough for me to turn and catch the outline of something snarling and lunging, drips of saliva clinging to sharp fangs.

A gasp rips me upright and I sit up. The stillness of my room makes my head swim, and it's a moment before I get my bearings. I was just outside, on the verge of being attacked. Now I'm in bed, in my room, seemingly having just woken from a dream. The balcony doors are closed, the sheer curtains still, and the night on the other side of the window thicker than oil. My covers drape over my lap, and my shaking hand pulls them off my legs. I glance around the room with distrustful eyes, not believing what I'm seeing.

I check the bottom of my feet only to see they're clean. No dirt or dust or grass from outside. No lingering taste of bread or yogurt or fruit, no matter how flavorless I remember them being. Nothing in my teeth to remind me of the food I know I ate. Instead, the image of blood pouring from Mina's body as I greedily lapped it up, of her tearing me apart to consume my very marrow, haunts my mind. My mouth waters with the vicious thoughts.

The digital clock on my nightstand reads three AM, and I immediately look at the door handle. It's going to be locked. It was last night. Two nights ago? My head spins as I try to make sense of the days. I press my hand to the side of my head to try and still it. I know Mina locks me in. Only when I shuffle across the room, still in my robe, I wrap my fingers around the handle and hear the telltale click of the door opening.

It creaks as it slowly swings in, exposing the dark hallway to me, lit only by a small lamp situated on a side table down the way. A quiet settles in the cave of the house, thick and soupy. There are no lights on outside, and no moonlight filters through the windows. Shielded by fog or absent entirely, I don't know.

Little Sister's—Gray Sky—is a different animal at night, closed off and protected. I feel like an interloper as I step into the hallway and take the stairs one at a time, my toes pressing lightly into the worn rug. My door was unlocked. That was Mina's rule. Obey locked doors. Now, there's nothing to obey.

Quiet settles thick on the main floor, the dark heavier here despite the large windows pointing out into the yard and to the cliffs beyond, shrouded in fog. A breeze flutters the gauzy curtains through an open window, but I barely feel the breath of it as I walk past, squinting through the shadows.

The house looms in the night. What is open and inviting in daylight hovers a sinister presence in the dark, its walls practically breathing. The house is a lung, inhaling my essence as I move through the hallways. I'm looking for something I can't name but searching all the same.

Around a corner, deep in the center of the house, a door stands ajar, soft light reaching through it. A door that was previously locked. I know because I tried them all. I had already opened the few I could, and that did not include this one. I step closer and the door creaks open wider, as if opening for me. An unlocked door with Mina's permission. It's an old cellar door. The one I found earlier with the padlock. It hangs in a loop on the back of the door, unlocked and tapping against the wood.

Something churns in my stomach, a twist of pain and the sharp pierce of hunger. My mouth waters with need, but the thought of eating anything nauseates me. Yet the hunger grows all-consuming.

Wooden stairs take me into a cave-like basement, thick with cobwebs and dust. Detritus clusters in corners—rotting boxes, ancient trunks, yellowed newspaper. Lives collected over the years. Mina's lives.

I turn off the stairs, and at the far side of the basement is another open door. Shadows slash across the light it offers as a tinkling laugh filters to my ears. A moan slides along behind it. A gasp. A squelch.

A coppery tang hits my nose, and my stomach groans with want. My gums ache, and I only have eyes for the open door. As I reach it, I tentatively peek inside, the crack just wide enough for me to sneak through if I so desired. My desire is strong but so is my fear as I see what's happening.

Two bodies lay spread out on the floor, their insides scattered about. Blood pools across the finished cement, an epoxy coating for easier cleaning, most likely. An anachronistic addition to this old house.

Aiden kneels in a pool of blood, naked, his cock as hard as his forearm, as Mina backs into him. His chest is bloody, his face smeared with it, and Mina rubs the clotted red fluid across her bare chest as she lowers herself onto him. But it's not her pussy he enters; it's her ass he slides into, inch by luscious inch as Mina throws her head back onto his shoulder and settles herself onto his body. Her bloodied hand grabs onto his chin, her fingers in his mouth. He sucks the blood from her digits as she writhes on him.

Once she's seated, she reaches in front of her. Another stark-naked man walks into view and kneels, no mind for the blood on the floor and covered in it himself. His thick curls are speckled with it.

Owen.

He takes his hardened shaft in his hand and strokes it a few times before pressing it between Mina's spread legs, entering her just as slowly as Aiden did. Her free hand lands on his shoulder as his hand holds her. Once he's seated, they move in tandem, this writhing organism covered in blood.

My pussy throbs at the sight of Mina getting fucked by two men. Moisture pools between my legs, dripping down my thigh. My insatiable hunger is met with a wave of desire so strong I nearly burst into the room and join them but manage to stand firm. The horror of the corpses around them, under them, of no mind to the fucking throuple.

Only it's not just three.

A third man enters my view, standing behind the pile of bodies and staring right at me. The familiarity of him overwhelms me. Confuses me. Until it clicks.

Nathaniel.

He's real.

Alive and just as young as the pictures from the eighteen hundreds. His hair is modern, dirty blond and disheveled. His body is lean but well-muscled, and he strokes his dick as he stares at me, a crooked smile across his face.

Until Caleb enters the picture, another naked body in that bloody room, and kneels in front of him to take Nathaniel's hard cock into his mouth. His head bobs in front of Nathaniel's body, and Nathaniel smiles and closes his eyes as his head rolls back. Mina's moans grow louder as Owen bites into a breast while Aiden sinks his teeth into her shoulder. They take a brief fill and pull away. Blood covers their faces as they lean toward each other, their mouths finding each other over Mina's body as they fuck her, before she grabs Owen's face and takes a kiss of her own. She runs her nails along Owen's shoulder, raking gouges into his flesh. She shudders with the motion and rides the two men harder. Aiden grabs tighter to Mina's body as he matches Owen's rhythm.

My fingers have slipped past the opening of my robe, the course, curly hair of my apex tickling my skin before I yank my hand away. Shame floods my veins. Right behind it is an insatiable desire I'm desperate to sate. A cacophony of moans grows louder as the bloody orgy continues, and I can't take my eyes from it. Horror at the eviscerated corpses strewn across the floor. At the amount of blood the murderers are fucking in. At the fangs in Mina's mouth. In Aiden's. In Nathaniel's.

Piercing pain rips through my mouth and I cry out, the noise a mix of pleasure and agony as my teeth throb. My tongue reaches for a tooth, and I gasp at the prick, the pain a sharp pierce and the metallic tang of blood a tease to my hunger.

Nathaniel pulls his head up, his eyes rolling forward as he looks at me. His gaze is sleepy and wanting, lost in the feeling of Caleb's mouth. His eyes grow more focused, his gaze more penetrating. The hairs on the back of my neck stand on end as fear slithers through the cracks of my desire, chipping away at its edges, reminding me of this house of horrors I'm standing in.

I inhale, this little gasp of air reminding me of the lungs in my chest. In that space of breath, Nathaniel stands next to me, the heady rot of blood thick on him as his fingers graze down my spine.

"Join us," he whispers, the soft tickle of his breath almost inviting until the smell of blood overwhelms me. "We've been waiting for you, Lucy. Less than patiently."

The slight curl of his lips wraps around the edges of his words, the smile sounding loud, but beneath it is the hiss of age. The wear of time as he walked through the centuries with Mina. Because of Mina most likely, and now he wants me to travel that same path.

From one blink to the next Mina stands in front of me, nothing but blood covering her body, caking her mouth. Much like my fever dream from the funhouse. We stand eye to eye, and she trails her fingers down my cheeks, runs her nail along my lip. Without saying a word, her hand travels down my arm until her fingers intertwine with mine. She pulls me forward, toward the death-filled room.

At first my feet follow hers with Nathaniel at my back, boxing me between them, Aiden, Owen, and Caleb waiting just beyond the door. Perhaps it's the banging of a pipe, or the settling of an old house, but something pulls me from my stupor. A sharp noise that slices through my psyche, knocking sense into my non-sensical head.

"No," I mutter, the word little more than a gasp. Until I find my voice. "No!"

It's a shout, a command. I rip my hand from Mina's grasp and twist away from Nathaniel before running back the way I came. Up the stairs, through the reaching shadows of the old Victorian, and out the front door. Wood presses into the soles of my feet as I dash across the porch, then stone as I step onto the pavers, and then dewy grass, the shocking chill slicing more reason across my mind. I don't think about where I'm running. I just run. My chin pulls over my shoulder, and I glance behind me. The crumbling monolith looms, shadows dark and reaching, before I pull my gaze forward again and keep running.

Fog envelops me, a chill mist settling into my bones as I lose myself in the low cloud. Soon enough there is no grass underfoot. No old Victorian behind me. No sky overhead. Just fog, thick and unyielding. Yet I run. I have no choice. Away is better than to them. They are not what I want. Not what I need. Perhaps if I repeat that to myself enough, it will come true. I try to find the gate, but the fog doesn't relent. In my terror at what I saw, a new one bubbles to the surface.

The cliff.

The thought alone stops me in my tracks. I can see barely

an arm's length in front of me. A single step can send me over the edge. Literally. My breaths come in great heaving gasps. My robe flutters in the slight breeze. What I don't hear, though, is the roaring ocean. No waves crashing into the bottom of the cliffs. No surf for me to plunge to my death in. The world is quiet, gray, and filled with an unending mist.

It's fuzzy, like my mind, blurring everything. Everything I've seen. Everything I've experienced. As if the fog wipes away the fantasy of my situation, giving me a clean slate. Perhaps this is all a dream. I'll wake up in my bed at Little Sister's again, sunlight streaming through the windows, and another day laid out before me. None of this will be real.

Please let it not be real, I tell myself just as another part of me thinks, *I'm desperate for this reality*.

I close my eyes against the thoughts, hold them in my mind as I listen for the world to wake up. For the waves to come roaring back in. For the creatures of the night to call out from the shadows, noises that scared me before, but I desperately miss now. Noises that rooted me in reality. As time drags on and my world stays muted, my concern grows. My worry. My panic that this is, indeed, real.

When I open my eyes I expect to find nothing but gray fog and muted grass beneath my feet. What greets me is the serene, bloodied face of Mina. Blood smears across her bare body, reminding me yet again of the funhouse. Finger streaks of red cross her nipples. There's a bite mark on her shoulder, the teeth wounds closing as I look at them.

Lush lips pull apart in a smile that bares elongated, sharpened teeth. My hand shoots to my own mouth, the ache still throbbing. The sharp stab of pain. My fingertips find razor points, and my stomach seeks to sate the growing hunger that swirls within it. My gaze trails the blood lines across Mina's body, and my mouth waters of its own volition, my tongue desperate to lick the bounty from her skin.

"You saw the ad, Lucy. You answered it." She shakes her head. "Only the truly lost see it, and even fewer stand where you are." She turns and motions behind her, back toward the house I can't see. "You've met them. You're meant to be part of our family. You found us, and we found you worthy."

Mina reaches out and pulls the pitiful tie of my robe. Its ends fall to my knees while the soft silk opens, exposing me to her. She steps forward and runs a finger down the center of me, between my breasts, over my naval, and down between my legs.

"You are ours," Mina whispers, as one finger plunges into me, then two, "and we are yours."

My breath hitches as her fingers wave inside of me. She steps forward, pressing her body against mine. The sweet smell of blood wafts to my nose, mingling with the scent of *her*. Like ocean air and the cotton candy sweetness of the boardwalk.

"You're killers," I mutter, as I try and fail to keep my focus on her. The rhythm of her fingers is too delicious to ignore.

"We are," she says, an unashamed agreement as she slides another finger into me.

An unabashed moan escapes my mouth, and I throw my head back as Mina fucks me. Her free hand clasps my waist and holds me to her. Without her, I'm afraid I would plummet into an abyss.

"Join us, Lucy. Let us show you what the world can really be."

My fingers trail across her skin, trace the blood patterns splattered there.

"Blood and death?" I groan, my voice a breathy whisper as I rest my forehead on her shoulder.

The scent of blood is overwhelming. My tongue wends its way out of my mouth and licks at a streak on her shoulder. Fireworks light up behind my eyes, like life must be pulled from the very molecules of the blood. As if this is the only way to truly experience life.

"Eternity," she whispers into my ear as she presses the side of her head against mine.

My orgasm mounts, blood rushing from my head as the foggy world swims. The ground underneath my feet tilts, and I wrap my arms tighter around Mina, holding her to me as if she were life itself. Her hand slides up my body, glances across a breast, and wraps around my throat. Her fingers gently squeeze as she pulls my head off her shoulder and holds me by the neck. My eyes lock on hers, my vision blurring as the orgasm overtakes me.

I throw my head back and howl, a primal yell as pleasure pulses through my body and nails bite into the flesh on my neck. A tongue, wet and warm, runs along the length of my throat before Mina pulls my head back down, my gaze landing on her.

The confinement of the cellar wraps around us, blood cloying the air as it lays pooled on the floor. Gone is the fog, the sterile nothingness of the night around Little Sister's. Blood puddles thick under my feet, between my bare toes as I step back, and back again, into waiting arms. Fingers wend around the silk robe and pull it the rest of the way from my body. Hands slide across my stomach, over my breasts, between my legs.

Mina sticks bloody fingers into her mouth and smiles as she watches me, watches her men swarm me. Caleb's gaze lingers on his master before he drags his eyes to me, a sly smile on his face. Permission granted. My blood sings for him. For all of them, and they don't disappoint.

"Welcome to your life, Lucy," Mina says, as she rubs a bloody finger across my lips before sliding the digit along my tongue.

Aiden wraps his arms around me from behind, one hand roughly grabbing a breast while the other squeezes my throat. He's much rougher than Mina, but the feeling is divine. My head swims and the feeling of falling rushes through me, yet Aiden holds me tight. I can still feel the mist brushing my skin, the bone-cold air whipping through my hair. But Aiden's warmth overpowers it. The sticky thickness of blood between my toes distracts me. Caleb steps between me and Mina, his hard length in one hand, and places it at my entrance, forcing me back to this exquisite moment. Mina beckons Owen and Nathaniel to her, and they come when called.

With one rough shove Caleb buries himself to the hilt in my cunt, and I cry out, a wave of pleasure washing over me, sudden and intense and all-consuming. Laugher fills my ears as pleasure fills my pussy, my ass, my mouth, my hands. Every piece of me consumed until there's nothing but depthless darkness and blood, and I welcome it all.

Re: I'M CALLING THE POLICE

To: QuinnMorrisEsq@helsinglaw.com
From: MAILER-DAEMON@nightshademail.com

I'm sorry to inform you that your message could not be delivered to recipient LucyWest87@nightshademail.com as sent. It is attached below. Error message reason: recipient could not be found. Please ensure there are no errors in the recipient's address and try again.

BY THE BLUFFS

Located upon the illustrious cliffs overlooking the healing waters of the grand Pacific Ocean, the luxurious Gray Sky Inn contains all the accoutremonts one could desire while convalescing amongst like-minds. All meals provided. A thrice-daily omnibus will transport riders to the seaside boardwalk to sample indulgent treats or peruse thrilling amusements. Pullman services from San Francisco daily and twice on week-ends.

WALTER PENNINGTON, OWNER AND MANAGER, SHADOW COVE, CA

SUBSCRIBE TO MY NEWSLETTER

If you liked what you read, then you definitely belong on my side of the book world! Sign up for my newsletter at rianadara books.com to stay up to date on my writing, book releases, and everything in between!

ACKNOWLEDGMENTS

This is such a weird book, and it would not exist without some weird folks supporting me along the way. And I mean that in the most loving way possible.

Thank you to Nico and Tiff for editing and providing feedback on this weird romp. Thank you to Drew Huff for designing the cover and capturing the book's weirdness in their amazing design. Thank you to Ash for being my guinea pig with this weirdo read, and for being one of my biggest cheerleaders. And thank you to Jess, Kay, and Hoot for helping me figure out where this puppy even belongs.

Thanks, of course, to my husband as he patiently waits for my spicy books to earn me enough to finally give him an allowance, and to my parents who will never, ever, *ever* read this book. Thank you to my IRL folks like Cass, who is the best hype person, and Eric for taking a chance on my books for his weirdo shop. Laura gets a mention, of course. This isn't a book she'll read. She hasn't built up her thick horror skin yet, but she will. I thank her all the same for sticking around.

And thank you to all my readers who love this kind of thing and encourage me to continue plumbing the depths of the dark corners of my mind for even more of this messed up stuff. Without your kind words, amazing reviews, and support, I'd honestly be too afraid to publish something like this. Thank you.

ABOUT THE AUTHOR

Rian Adara is a multi-genre author who has a deep love of morally gray (or black) characters, writing with a hint (or a lot) of darkness, and varying levels of spice. She enjoys destroying her readers with her words and riling them up at the same time. And may or may not derive joy from creeping them out too. When she's not writing she's reading, paper-crafting, taking moody photos, wrangling her cats, and spending time with her husband. The gothic aesthetic of New England will always be considered home, no matter where she lives.

You can find her on her website, www.rianadarabooks.com, or at @rianadarabooks at Instagram, Threads, and Pinterest.